Bokuto
Uno

ILLUSTRATION BY

Ruria
Miyuki

I

Reign
of the **SEVEN**
SPELLBLADES

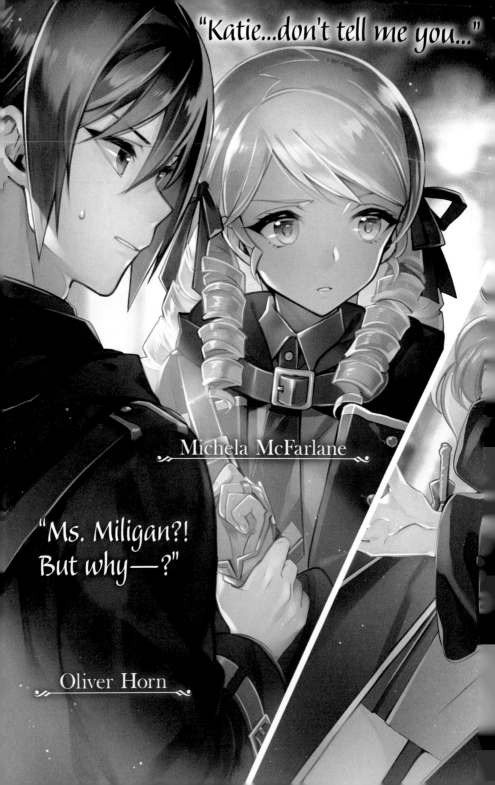

Katie Aalto

Vera Miligan

"One suicide or two—
that's the only difference
in your plans."

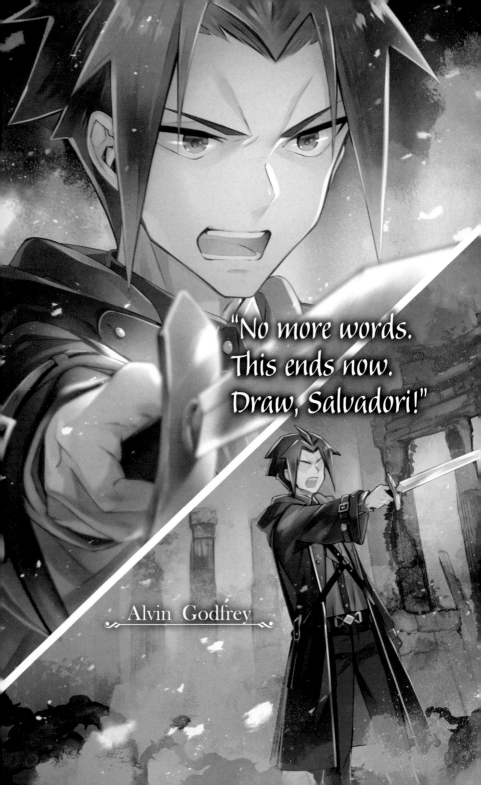

"No more words.
This ends now.
Draw, Salvadori!"

Alvin Godfrey

"...Your heart has been stained by the labyrinth's darkness, too."

Ophelia Salvadori

Nanao Hibiya

CONTENTS

Reign of the Seven Spellblades
Bokuto Uno

Reign of the SEVEN SPELLBLADES

III

Bokuto Uno

ILLUSTRATION BY
Ruria Miyuki

YEN
ON

New York

Reign of the Seven Spellblades, Vol. 3
Bokuto Uno

Translation by Alex Keller-Nelson
Cover art by Ruria Miyuki

NANATSU NO MAKEN GA SHIHAISURU Vol. 3
©Bokuto Uno 2019
Edited by Dengeki Bunko
First published in Japan in 2019 by KADOKAWA CORPORATION, Tokyo.
English translation rights arranged with KADOKAWA CORPORATION, Tokyo
through TUTTLE-MORI AGENCY, INC., Tokyo.

English translation © 2021 by Yen Press, LLC

Yen On
150 West 30th Street, 19th Floor
New York, NY 10001

Visit us at yenpress.com
facebook.com/yenpress
twitter.com/yenpress
yenpress.tumblr.com
instagram.com/yenpress

First Yen On Edition: August 2021

Yen On is an imprint of Yen Press, LLC.
The Yen On name and logo are trademarks of Yen Press, LLC.

Library of Congress Cataloging-in-Publication Data
Names: Uno, Bokuto, author. | Ruria, Miyuki, illustrator. | Keller-Nelson, Alexander,
translator.
Title: Reign of the seven spellblades / Bokuto Uno ; illustration by Miyuki Ruria ;
translation by Alex Keller-Nelson.
Other titles: Nanatsu no maken ga shihai suru. English
Description: First Yen On edition. | New York, NY : Yen On, 2020–
Identifiers: LCCN 2020041085 | ISBN 9781975317195 (v. 1 ; trade paperback) | ISBN
9781975317201 (v. 2 ; trade paperback) | ISBN 9781975317225 (v. 3 ; trade paperback)
Subjects: CYAC: Fantasy. | Magic—Fiction. | Schools—Fiction.
Classification: LCC PZ7.1.U56 Re 2020 | DDC [Fic]—dc23
LC record available at https://lccn.loc.gov/2020041085

ISBNs: 978-1-9753-1722-5 (paperback)
978-1-9753-1723-2 (ebook)

1 3 5 7 9 10 8 6 4 2

LSC-C

Printed in the United States of America

Characters

Reign of the Seven Spellblades

First-Years

Oliver Horn

The story's protagonist. Jack-of-all-trades, master of none. Swore revenge on the seven instructors who killed his mother.

Nanao Hibiya

A samurai girl from Azia. Believes that Oliver is her destined sword partner.

A girl from Farnland, a nation belonging to the Union. Has a soft spot for the civil rights of demi-humans.

Katie Aalto

A boy from a family of magical farmers. Honest and friendly. Has a knack for magical flora.

Guy Greenwood

A studious boy born to nonmagicals. Capable of switching between male and female bodies. Was captured by a monster and is currently missing.

Pete Reston

Eldest daughter of the prolific McFarlane family. A master of the pen and sword, she looks out for her friends.

Michela McFarlane

A lone wolf who taught himself the sword by ignoring the fundamentals. Lost to Oliver in a duel.

Tullio Rossi

Richard Andrews

Heir of the Andrews nobility. Currently searching for a new purpose in life after fighting Oliver and Nanao.

Stacy Cornwallis

A girl born to a McFarlane branch family. Michela's younger half sister.

Fay Willock

A half-werewolf taken in by Stacy. Serves as her attendant.

Joseph Albright

An arrogant boy born to the militaristic Albright family. Lost to Oliver in a duel.

Fourth-Years

Vera Miligan

A witch who supports demi-human rights. Fought Oliver and his friends over Katie but has since taken an interest in the group.

Ophelia Salvadori

A witch who carries chimeras in her womb. After perfecting her magecraft, she has been "consumed by the spell."

Fifth-Years

Alvin Godfrey

Student council president. Nicknamed Purgatory by his peers. Boasts incredible firepower.

Carlos Whitrow

An androgynous youth with a beautiful voice. Ophelia's childhood friend.

Gwyn Sherwood

A quiet young man and Oliver's cousin. Supports Oliver's secret activities as his vassal.

Cyrus Rivermoore

A necromancer who controls the bones of the dead. Equally as dangerous as Ophelia.

Shannon Sherwood

A gentle girl and Oliver's cousin. Supports Oliver's secret activities as his vassal.

Sixth-Years

Kevin Walker

President of the Labyrinth Gourmet Club. Survived in the labyrinth for half a year, earning him the nickname the Survivor.

Instructors

Kimberly's headmistress. Proudly stands at the apex of magical society.

Esmeralda

Magical biology instructor. Feared by her students for her wild personality.

Vanessa Aldiss

Alchemy instructor. Slain by Oliver and currently considered missing.

Darius Grenville

- Frances Gilchrist
- Enrico Forghieri
- Luther Garland
- Dustin Hedges
- Theodore McFarlane

Others

- Teresa Carste
- Marco

Her personal rule was to spend sunny days out in the garden until she was summoned back inside.

It wasn't something she particularly enjoyed, however. The garden never changed throughout the seasons, nor did she exactly care for flowers. In fact, she hated them. Their eye-catching beauty and heavenly scents that attracted all manner of insects reminded her too much of herself.

"…"

She stomped them all under her feet—a brief catharsis.

Once she'd had her fill, she looked up at the sky and took a deep breath. The wall, overgrown with moss, normally blocked out the sun. But at noon, the sun's rays were relentless. Soaking in that light was the greatest respite she could ask for. She enjoyed it while she could; she had to. Once her belly got bigger, it would be impossible to even walk around in the garden.

The house was too dark, too fetid—too many things crawled within the darkness. She'd always been afraid that one day, she would become one of them.

"Good day. Nice weather we're having."

A voice snapped her out of her enjoyment of her temporary peace. It was calm, neutral, and unlike any voice she knew. Suspicious, she turned around to find a thin boy she'd never seen before standing there.

"…Who are you?"

"I could be a friend, if you like."

He strode briskly through the garden with the most natural of

movements, taking care not to step on a single flower. When he stood before her, she glared up at him and sighed lightly.

"Am I going to bear your child this time?"

She asked merely to confirm, expecting nothing but an affirmation. It was difficult to think of another role for any male within the mansion's grounds. Shockingly, however, he didn't nod. Instead, he grinned wryly.

"Oh, no, honey. That's not possible for me."

"…? What the heck?"

Unable to understand what he was saying, she felt the suspicion in her gaze mounting. He smiled and shrugged, as if to try and placate her.

"But enough of that. So did you want someone to chat with or not, Princess Grumpy?"

His gaze flicked to the ground where she stood—to the dirt-covered flowers she'd trampled. She turned away, pouting, feeling like a criminal who had been caught in the act.

"There's no point. You're male, aren't you? They all go crazy after talking to me."

"I can promise I won't, love."

His face swooped in close to hers, and her shoulders twitched. She'd never seen a male who had maintained his sanity after getting so near to her.

"…!"

She was sure he was going to attack her and instinctively stiffened—but nothing happened, no matter how long she waited. Strangely, the boy was still merely standing there.

"See? Nothing."

"……"

Her eyes widened from the shock. The boy took her right hand, wrapped his palm around it, and smiled brightly.

"There, now we're friends. Can I call you Lia?"

*   *   *

"Mm…"

She opened her eyes, got up, and looked sleepily around. Nearby was a teacup, its contents long gone cold. Alchemic catalysts littered the surface of the desk she'd fallen asleep on as the small chimeras in charge of housework busily shuffled about the messy workshop, which was in even more disarray than normal. This was her base, which she'd used to full effect for about three years since obtaining it at the beginning of her second year of school. From time to time, she brought in prey that she'd Charmed, but she'd never once invited in a guest. This had become Ophelia's new world ever since she'd decided to distance herself from the academy's surface.

"…Ironic, dreaming of them at a time like this."

Her lips twisted in self-derision. She rose from her chair and instantly toppled over.

"*Pant… Pant…!*"

She'd let her guard down for only a second, yet that was enough for her reason to completely slip. Desperately suppressing the blaze rising from her abdomen like a fierce, starving beast, Ophelia felt her breathing become ragged.

"…Not yet. Not yet… I still need to keep my wits about me…"

Shakily, she stood and dragged her listless body forward. She downed an infusion that would temporarily stabilize her mind—and suddenly, she remembered the job she'd ordered her familiars to do. She moved to the neighboring room to check on the fruits of their labor.

"Hmm…?" she uttered softly.

Before her was a lattice of pulsating flesh that formed a living prison. A number of underclassmen lay limp inside. This sight caused her no surprise, but among the innocent-looking boys, she spotted a familiar bespectacled student. She sighed.

"…That Mr. Horn—I warned him about going on adventures."

But there was nothing to be done about it now. Without any further emotion, she silently turned around.

Kimberly hadn't seen a state of alert like this in a full year. It was evening, and the campus had suddenly dissolved into madness. A group of prefects, the students charged with keeping the peace on school grounds, marched through the academy halls.

"Prepare to descend. Ready, Carlos?" Alvin Godfrey, aka Purgatory and head prefect, asked from his position at the front. A blond youth, eyes flickering with unease, responded.

"Of course, President. We're the Kimberly Student Council. We're always prepared to cross into the realm of death."

The youth cracked their knuckles loudly. Tightly packed vials of potion threatened to burst out of the pouch at their waist. The other prefects swallowed. There was enough potion to easily kill ten thousand people without fail. The apprehensive blond youth's neighbor, a dark-skinned girl with sharp eyes, spoke up.

"Our reputation will take a hit if we don't act now. But most of all, we're to blame for this incident. Don't you agree, Godfrey?"

Godfrey nodded curtly. Next to him, the stunningly androgynous Carlos Whitrow cut in. "Tim and Sedi are right. We're ready and waiting. Let's go."

They had all prepared for this day. Godfrey ground his teeth. "Unfortunately, we lost the initiative… Things happened much quicker than I expected. I'd hoped for another year, at the least."

"She must have sensed our plans and accelerated hers. She was always a pusher, that one," Carlos said affectionately despite the dire situation. Godfrey fumed silently. Carlos then whispered into Godfrey's ear as they walked.

"If I fail…the rest is up to you, Al."

"……"

After a long pause, Godfrey nodded slightly. Carlos smiled. Eventually, the group stopped their march in front of a giant mirror.

"Shall we, then? On to our final adventure."

Carlos, somewhat gleefully, extended their hand toward the mirror without hesitation. The reflective surface rippled as it swallowed the youth. The others nodded to one another and followed close behind.

CHAPTER 1

Possibility of Survival

It was eleven o'clock in the morning when the temperature dropped oddly low and freezing rain began to pour outside. A group of first-years was seated in one classroom, listening anxiously. Meanwhile, their ancient instructor's voice was stern and completely unaffected by current events.

"...Mages who dedicate themselves to magical duels often lose sight of the true nature of spells. Speaking quickly, shortening casts as much as possible—consider such behavior cause for alarm."

It was standard for their instructor, Frances Gilchrist, to start every class with nagging warnings. The witch put a huge emphasis on a healthy respect for spells. Techniques lacking this respect were to be avoided at all costs, regardless of effectiveness.

"Only in magical duels does battling over meager seconds and finishing a cast first result in a victory. Furthermore, battles are just a tiny part of a mage's business. If any of you pride yourselves in the quickness of your casting, I urge you to amend your thinking now. Lest you end up like Badderwell."

"......"

Badderwell was a sorcerer famed for the speed of his spells, and yet, in the end, he was done in by an average swordsman. Of course, Oliver understood that Badderwell's fate was an important lesson that must be taught. The elderly witch was entirely correct. But right now, that "correctness" was what ate him up the most.

"Proper enunciation, careful mental imagery: These are the main principles of spellcasting. Without them, haste makes waste. Even the basic fire spells you all take for granted can be quite a different animal with proper focus…"

This lecture was centered on the next ten years. Oliver balled his fists in uncontrollable irritation. It was *now* that he desired power, *now* that his friend was crying out for help.

"…Pete still hasn't come back…," Guy muttered, his plate piled high with untouched food. The silence was painful. It wasn't just their table, either—for the past few days, the characteristic boisterousness of the Fellowship had been replaced by an eerie hush.

"…President Godfrey and the other upperclassmen are doing their best to rescue the abducted. All we can do is have faith in them and wait," said Chela.

"It's been *days* now."

Chela's statement caused Guy to smack his plate irritably with his fork. Oliver chewed his lip.

"Like, are the prefects even trying? He's gonna starve at this rate!"

"…He's not the only one, Guy. I suggest you eat, too," Chela offered. "What happened to the boy who could give Nanao a run for her money at the dinner table?"

"How'm I supposed to have an appetite when my friend's been kidnapped?!"

Guy slammed his fist onto the table, angry and bitter that he couldn't join the effort to help his friend. Pete was Oliver's friend as well, but Oliver tried his best to stay cool.

"Easy, Guy. There's nothing we can do. Right now…we can't help."

But despite his efforts, Oliver was practically screaming in anguish. The two boys were equally frustrated by their powerlessness.

His emotions coming to a boil, Guy shouted, "Then you shoulda let me get taken, too! At least if we were together, I could cook Pete something!"

"Cease this line of thinking, Guy. You cannot eat if you're dead."

The Azian girl's voice was stony as she solemnly proceeded with her meal. Guy rounded on her.

"...What the hell is that supposed to mean, Nanao?"

"Precisely what it sounded like. If you or Pete perish, then the only food you will ever see are the offerings at your grave."

"You think Pete's dead?!"

"I cannot say. However, in my home village, the vast majority of those who went missing on the battlefield were found as corpses."

Guy was dumbstruck; Katie's shoulders quivered. Unwilling to let this go, Oliver interjected.

"You're being too pessimistic, Nanao. From what I could see, it was designed to capture its targets without killing them. There must be a reason its master wanted Pete alive. If we can figure that out, the chances of him surviving skyrocket."

As he spoke, Oliver began to lose confidence in how much of what he was saying was speculation and how much was sheer hope. The group fell silent again, until Katie muttered something from the end of the table.

"What...would this terrible person want with Pete, then?"

The silence grew heavier. No one could come up with an answer. Chela, who had been eating almost robotically, quietly got to her feet.

"...It's time. I'm heading to our next class."

"Hey! Wait, Chela—!"

"There is no point in arguing among ourselves here."

She cut Guy off curtly and strode away. He looked at the floor and gritted his teeth; her words were cold, but she was undoubtedly correct.

The more he thought about it, the more evident it became: If they were powerless, then their only option was to rely on someone who could accomplish what they couldn't.

"Noll?"

The academy's third-story lounge hardly ever saw first-years. But, as if predicting his visit, Oliver's cousins were there waiting. Gwyn shot him a look. Aware of the upperclassmen's stares, Oliver approached his cousin's table.

"Allow me to be direct, Brother: Could you help in rescuing Pete?"

Oliver cut to the chase; there was no need to bring them up to speed on the situation, as he'd already explained everything the other day.

Instantly, Shannon's face fell. Gwyn placed a fresh cup of tea in front of Oliver, then responded calmly.

"If you're asking us to join in the search, then we've already been assisting President Godfrey for three days now at his request. But in all honestly...progress has been poor. Salvadori's territory is on the third level of the labyrinth. If she truly wished to hide, finding her wouldn't be easy, to put it mildly."

Oliver remained silent. He'd expected this answer. Of course the prefects had already tapped any upperclassmen willing to help in the search-and-rescue effort. Yet, still, they hadn't found a thing. A witch hiding in the depths of the labyrinth could be a slippery prey— that much was crystal clear.

"We cannot mobilize our allies in this situation. You understand why...yes?" Gwyn added in a hush so that only Oliver could hear, speaking not as his senior but as his vassal. Oliver silently signaled his understanding. Their connection and plans couldn't afford to be exposed yet.

"Don't beat yourself up, Noll. I'm doing my best to help, too, okay?"

Shannon reached out and gently placed her hand on his tightly balled fist. Oliver stared down at his reflection in the tea. All he saw looking back at him was a weak little boy.

Naturally, Oliver wasn't the only one going around begging for help. That day, as soon as their sword arts lesson was over, a girl's shriek echoed through the vast classroom.

"Please! Please save Pete!" Katie begged, nearly in hysterics.

Master Garland, their sword arts instructor, looked at her completely unperturbed. His face was as stiff as a mask, without a hint of his usual friendliness.

"I'm sorry, but I can't. That's an academy rule, Ms. Aalto. The staff can only intervene when the situation has become too much for students to handle. In Mr. Reston's case, we are not at that stage yet."

"'*Yet*'? We have no idea what he's being put through! What will it take for you to help, then?!" Katie demanded, livid. After a few seconds, Garland answered firmly.

"The rule is that staff may begin searching for students lost in the labyrinth after eight days have passed."

"'*E-eight days*'?!"

Her eyes went wide with shock at the completely unexpected and unreasonable number. Garland seemed to understand her anger.

"It's because the possibility of survival drops dramatically after that point. It sounds cruel, but the academy doesn't want its students to go around thinking the staff will bail them out of any jam they find themselves in. Under Kimberly's system, that would only lead to even further tragedies. Your life and death are your own responsibility. That's what the headmistress told you at the entrance ceremony. This is one of those times."

His decision was final. Katie was completely rebuffed; her shoulders trembled, and her head hung low.

"...I understand."

She excused herself and turned around. Her hopes of getting an instructor to help were gone. Instead, her eyes now burned with resolve.

"So we have to figure this out on our own, then."

Oliver arrived at their usual dinner table to find only Nanao sitting there. Still feeling glum, he sat next to her and began eating, though his heart wasn't in it.

"'Ello there. Strange times we live in, eh, Oliver?"

Almost instantly, someone called out to him from behind. Oliver raised his hand limply but didn't turn around. There was no mistaking that unique accent. Tullio Rossi, still nursing a loss from their duel in the labyrinth the other day, strode over and stood right next to Oliver.

"I am sure you 'ave already noticed, but the battle royale is on 'old. The whole academy is in a tizzy from the state of emergency. Not a good time for first-years to be cavorting about, no? Too bad… Albright, Willock, and even Pete got kidnapped, eh? Did I hear that right?"

Oliver didn't feel like engaging him, so he just gave a short nod. Rossi studied him for a bit, then snorted.

"No need to look so down in the dumps…'ere, a piece of advice: You had better not get any ideas—like going to rescue Pete yourself."

Oliver responded with more silence. After all this time, there was no way he *hadn't* thought of that once or twice. But Rossi knew this, and he continued.

"This is nothing like our little squabbles between first-years. That girl is a Salvadori. The upperclassmen searching for 'er are risking their *lives*, no? So what the hell can you and your little friends do? Not that I am in any place to lecture you, though."

"……"

"Besides, you and Pete 'ave not known each other very long. No use getting chummy with others. People can lose their lives anytime at Kimberly; you must get used to letting people go, or you will only 'urt yourself more."

For those who lived at Kimberly, there was no arguing with this line of reasoning. Oliver gritted his teeth and stared at his plate.

Rossi sighed, then turned around. "I 'ad a feeling you would not appreciate my meddling, eh? But you know—I would not like to see you killed so quickly. I would be so *bored*."

And with that, he disappeared into the dining hall crowd. Oliver felt pathetic; his nails dug into the tablecloth. Did he really look so desperate that even a snake like Rossi felt the need to comfort him?

"...Oliver, do you have a moment?"

After leaving Nanao in the dining hall, Oliver wandered the halls alone until a voice called out to him. He turned around to see Chela, her expression stony.

"Yeah, sure—"

"Over here."

She urged him toward a more secluded spot. They stopped in a corner, and Chela spoke again.

"First, I have some bad news. We cannot expect help from the staff. At least, not for another five days."

"...Did you talk to Instructor McFarlane?"

"Yes. I even blatantly tried to use my position as his daughter to make him act." She paused for a second, shoulders quivering. "My father said, *If you haven't the power to protect them, then the moment you make a friend is also the moment you lose them. That's life here at Kimberly.*"

"......"

Oliver couldn't think of anything to say. Chela must have been similarly struck speechless when her father had said those words. Oliver remained silent, but Chela lifted her head.

"I thought I should inform you—I'm heading into the labyrinth tonight," she announced.

"—?!"

Oliver could hardly believe his own ears. But Chela's eyes were brimming with determination, and he realized there could be no mistaking her.

"Are you crazy, Chela? That's suicide."

"I know. Naturally, I'll be asking seniors for help first. Many of the

students here have ties to the McFarlanes in some way, so I'm sure I'll
be able to find someone to assist me."

Chela tried to explain that she wasn't going blindly to her grave. She
might not be able to rely on her father, Theodore, but she had a good
number of connections on campus. Oliver was aware of this. But he
still objected.

"That's just one more reason to leave this to the upperclassmen,
then. You said so earlier."

"…When Pete was captured, it was me who stopped you from going
back to help him. I bear some responsibility for this situation."

"Don't be ridiculous! Things were different then. I should be the
one—"

He raised his voice, but Chela pressed her index finger over his lips,
silencing him.

"Listen to me. That was…a calculation."

"…A what?"

"I was weighing the risk of going back to help him and getting all
of us killed, versus our chances of survival if we abandoned him. I
couldn't devise an effective way to deal with that chimera. The one
tiny detail I could glimpse was that it was created to capture its prey
alive. I assumed it wouldn't immediately kill Pete."

She revealed what had gone through her mind that night—the panic
of seeing her friends in danger and the cold, calculating kernel of logic
that every grown mage possessed deep within.

"The best solution I could come up with at the time was to escape
the labyrinth with as few casualties as possible, then summon the
upperclassmen for help. Thus, I obviously couldn't let you go back. If
you went, Nanao would follow. And the others as well, I assume."

Oliver couldn't deny this. It was the same reason he'd stopped, too.

"I considered our chances if we all worked together, but the risk of
us dying seemed much greater. It wasn't just that one chimera down
there. We could've been caught by other beasts while trying to save

Pete and the others or have our path cut off and become trapped... So many disasters ran through my mind, and so vividly."

She finished her speech calmly, then hung her head low. Oliver, who had been cowed into silence, noticed her shoulders quaking.

"And—I weighed the value of our friend's life."

Her voice was dripping with self-loathing and regret. Oliver swallowed. Chela had acted the calmest among all of them since Pete's kidnapping—but the truth was, she was the most tortured by it.

"Please let me take make up for my mistake. Otherwise, I'll never be able to look Pete in the eye again."

This will be my penance, she implied. There was no way he could just sit by and watch her do this. His thoughts still jumbled, Oliver instinctively replied, "...I'm coming, too."

"No you're not. If you don't stay, the other three will immediately come after us into the labyrinth."

She shook her head, holding back the rest of the message: *I'm not going to drag anyone else to their death.* However...

"...Oh—"

...it was pointless to try and convince her using words, so Oliver grabbed her by the wrists. Chela seemed flustered, but he gripped harder so as to keep hold. He locked her wavering eyes with his.

"I'm not letting you go alone," he practically shouted. "Not on my life!"

"Oliver..."

Chela stood completely still, a mixture of sadness and longing spread over her face. Both at a loss for words, simply feeling the warmth of each other's skin, a long silence fell over them.

"One suicide or two—that's the only difference in your plans."

A totally unexpected voice broke the silence. Surprised, Oliver and Chela turned to the source to find a stressed-looking, curly-haired girl and, standing next to her, an upperclassman with a kindly smile— Vera Miligan.

"Ms. Miligan?! But why—?"

"Yes, why indeed?" Miligan's gaze flicked to her side, and Katie looked away awkwardly. Chela, putting the pieces together, glared at her.

"Katie…don't tell me you…"

"……"

Katie's silence spoke volumes.

In her stead, the Snake-Eyed Witch explained dryly, "'*You can experiment on my body all you want—just save my friend!*' Boy, you guys sure have a tight-knit group, don't you? It's too pure for my evil eye to behold."

It was about what he'd imagined. Oliver fixed Katie with a withering stare.

"You're selling your body, Katie?!"

"…I am, if it means I can save my friend."

"Katie… Honestly, what am I going to do with you…?" Dizzy, Chela held her forehead in her hand.

Oliver glared at the Snake-Eyed Witch. "I'm sorry, Ms. Miligan, but I need you to decline her request right now."

"Oliver! This was *my* decision!"

"Yeah, I know. You made it all on your own, without consulting any of us!"

He made no effort to hide his anger, and Katie's voice caught in her throat. Miligan, however, didn't seem bothered by the tension in the air.

"I figured this would happen," she said. "But really—what exactly do you have planned? None of you intends on abandoning your friend. You're all set on going to save Pete, no matter what methods you have to employ. Correct?"

"……"

Oliver bit his lip. He knew all too well the pain that had driven Katie to make her rash decision. They couldn't sit on the sidelines or hesitate anymore. Pete could be crying out for help this very second.

"You have good intentions, but I don't like your chances," Miligan continued. "President Godfrey and any upperclassmen amicable to the cause have already been mobilized to bring the situation under control. You kids don't have what it takes to act like heroes. That said, *I'm* heading into the labyrinth tonight."

Reality shoved in their faces, the three friends fell silent. Miligan shrugged. "Let's just talk this out. For better or worse, I still owe you guys for the thing with Katie. I can lend an ear for free."

The witch attempted to placate them.

Oliver shared a look with Chela and, after some slight hesitation, took her up on her offer. "...What do you think is the best way to increase Pete's chances of survival?"

He'd been so focused on saving Pete, he'd put no thought into *how*. Now acutely aware of his mistake, he sought an answer from Miligan. She crossed her arms and pondered.

"Hmm, good question... The safest option would be to not interfere with the students already involved with the rescue effort. They won't let anyone murder a lowerclassman without a fight. I'm sure they're doing their best to bring everyone home safely."

"...I don't deny that. However, even if we leave everything up to them, what are the chances they succeed, in your opinion?" Chela asked, cursing her own ineffectiveness.

Miligan thought for a few seconds. "Depends on how you interpret the situation. If you're asking how likely it is that the abductees are still alive, even after all this time, the odds are quite good. But if you include the fact that they were kidnapped, especially by a student consumed by the spell—well, that changes things quite a bit."

Oliver figured as much. This was way more complicated than a simple accident.

"You can probably come up with some numbers based on past cases, but each one is so different that the calculations won't mean much. If you really want to determine Pete's odds of survival, you have to fully analyze whatever state he currently finds himself in."

Katie and Chela fell into thought. She had a point—Oliver agreed. That was one of the first things they needed to determine: What exactly was Pete dealing with? What were the dangers?

"...Ophelia Salvadori is in your year, isn't she?" Oliver asked, lifting his head as he remembered this fact. The Snake-Eyed Witch smiled.

"Good deduction. Yes, I do in fact know her. Unfortunately, we weren't what you'd call friends, but I can still imagine what's going on with her at the moment."

The three friends looked at Miligan with hope in their eyes as she laid her knowledge upon them.

"And if we use that to calculate Pete's chances of survival...we get twenty percent, at best," she stated flatly.

"""......!"""

"Salvadori has no reason to let Pete leave alive, nor even the presence of mind to consider it. Consumed by the spell as she is, she will be using every tool at her disposal in order to further her research. Nothing is above sacrificing for her. She'll be burning through her abductees as if they grow on trees."

Oliver and the girls stared at their feet and gritted their teeth, trying to fight off the overwhelming sense of despair. Most of what Miligan was saying was pure speculation, and yet, it hit with surprising force. Their hope of seeing Pete come back alive was fading fast. Then, as if waiting for just the right moment, Miligan continued.

"I say twenty percent because I can imagine *how* she's using those lives, too. The field of research Ophelia specializes in doesn't require her to immediately kill them. Their use isn't as sacrifices but as fuel."

They realized the meaning behind this comparison—in both cases, the subject would be killed, but in the latter one, it would take time to fully burn up.

"You get it, don't you? It's a race to see if Godfrey and the other prefects can save them in time. Not only do they have to play hide-

and-seek in the vast labyrinth, but there's no denying the disadvantage playing catch-up means for them. Salvadori's been carefully planning this for a while."

"Then even more so, they should welcome as many helping hands as possible. Does our involvement not increase Pete's chances of survival, in your opinion?" Chela asked, a hand to her chest in concern.

But Miligan immediately shook her head. "I can't see it. In fact, it likely *lowers* his survival rate. If you kids do something reckless and end up in danger, the rescue team will have to divert resources in order to help you."

"……"

Chela bit her lip and looked at the floor. She couldn't argue with the accusation of being powerless, and her two friends were no different.

"However, if you can manage to not get in the way, that 20 percent chance of victory could turn into a 20.1 percent chance."

Their heads rose instantly in unison at this. Oliver studied Miligan's impish smile with suspicion.

"…What does that mean?"

"I'm saying you have some hope, depending on your training. This is just my opinion, of course." The witch looked at Oliver and Chela for a second, then closed her eyes. "Let's change the subject. Truth be told, my research has reached a dead end."

The sudden confession shocked them. Miligan continued with a note of bitterness in her voice. "But I guess that much is obvious. Now that my endless source of demi-humans is gone, I can't keep using my past methods. Instructor Darius took care of all my needs, but he's gone missing. President Godfrey is also on my ass thanks to our previous incident. My hands are basically tied no matter what I want to do."

Oliver was racked with anxiety, but he didn't let even a hair on his head fall out of place. *Stay calm*, he told himself. Darius Grenville was a Kimberly instructor, and the importance of his position meant his disappearance would affect many parts of the academy. Naturally, Miligan, who had been receiving his support, would reference this.

"Luckily, there is a bright side. See, I also have an interest in interspecies communication studies, just as Katie does. You all remember the final key to the success of the intellectualization of our troll friend, don't you?"

Marco the troll, who'd been placed under Katie's care, popped into their minds. They'd gotten separated in the labyrinth, and none of them had any idea if he was okay. After Miligan had messed with his brain, it was only thanks to Katie's devoted attempts at communication that he learned to speak the human tongue, creating a trusting relationship that crossed barriers.

"So in the interest of digging into a new field, I offered Katie a position as my coresearcher. That's why I gave her an entire workshop, as a sort of foundation to build upon. I wanted to come off as a kind, generous mentor."

Her frank manner made Oliver furrow his brow. Talk about shameless. Did she forget about how she'd kidnapped Katie and tried to split open her skull?

"Which is why even if you hadn't stopped her, Oliver, I would have shot down Katie's idea anyway. It would be such a waste to only be able to pick your brain once you're dead." The Snake-Eyed Witch grinned and paused. A moment later, she continued. "So here's my proposal—I'll train you all until you're at least able to assist the rescue effort. Of course, I'll also help you search for Pete and guide you through the labyrinth."

Three sets of eyes stared at her in disbelief. Oliver and his friends mulled over Miligan's unexpected offer.

"In exchange, once this situation is taken care of, Katie will become my coresearcher."

"...Huh?" Katie squeaked in surprise at the added condition.

Oliver stepped in before she could follow up. "...By *'coresearcher,'* what exactly do you mean?" he demanded.

"Quite literally, we'll be comrades researching the same field," Miligan replied. "Oftentimes this entails a teacher-student relationship, but in this case, we'll be equals. I have zero experience in this field, you see. Of course, we'll perform our research together, and Katie will be able to learn from my expertise if it becomes relevant. The only thing limiting her will be her own willingness and the amount of effort she puts in. So what do you think of that? No need to sell any bodies, right? Plus, this deal benefits both sides greatly."

"I accept!" Katie immediately raised her hand, looking at Oliver and Chela. "I'm not going to let you stop me! This is a good deal—you have to see that!"

Her fearsome gaze brooked no argument. Oliver put up his hands in a show of submission. "Calm down, Katie. You're right—it sounds like a good deal. *Too* good... Ms. Miligan, have you really told us everything you're after?"

He locked eyes with the Snake-Eyed Witch as he expressed his doubts. He wasn't about to take a deal like this at face value—not at Kimberly, and especially not coming from Vera Miligan.

"If you're asking if I have ulterior motives, then sure I do. Lots of them, in fact. But you'll have to figure that out on your own. Don't blindly trust me—calculate the risk versus return, then decide if this deal fits your needs. That's what a transaction between mages is like."

She lectured them like the inexperienced mages they were; Oliver's and Chela's expressions hardened as they considered her offer. She was right, of course. All mages harbored secrets. It wouldn't do to simply place their hopes in her good intentions—they had to be prepared to read into every last detail to get a peek behind the curtain.

"......"

And so Oliver searched for a motive. What did Miligan stand to gain from this deal, besides an improvement in her relationship with Katie?

"…This allows you to get closer to Nanao, too, doesn't it?"

He confidently mentioned the first thing that came to mind. Chela and Katie seemed confused, but Miligan—who had experienced Nanao's spellblade personally—curled the corners of her lips into a playful smile. Bull's-eye.

"Not that I'd be able to get up to anything naughty with you around," Miligan said and shrugged, then got back on topic. "Keep in mind," she added, "even should you accept, there's no guarantee that Pete will make it back alive. There's no guarantee *you'll* make it back alive, either."

As scary as it sounded, this seemed like a sincere warning to Oliver and Chela. After all, they were trying to rescue their friend from *the* Ophelia Salvadori. Of course they would be risking their lives.

"But it still gives us a chance! …Let's do it! Oliver, Chela—let's save Pete!"

Katie, her mind totally set, pushed her two friends to join her. Miligan, however, dumped water on her fire.

"Sorry to burst your bubble, Katie, but you can't come with us."

"What?!"

"To be brutally honest, you're too green. Any lower than the second layer and you'll just get in the way. I'll be taking Mr. Horn, Ms. McFarlane, and Ms. Hibiya, and that's not up for discussion."

Katie was dumbfounded by the sudden ostracizing. Oliver and Chela looked at each other, thought for a bit, then both nodded.

"…All right."

"No objections."

"Whaaaat?! W-wait a second! This was *my* idea!"

"Easy, Katie," said Miligan. "We still need you to hold down the fort here. Traveling to the third layer isn't some weekend trip. Your friends will need someone to take notes for them in class."

Miligan placed a hand gently on Katie's shoulder and tried to soothe her.

Oliver joined in. "Sorry, Katie, but can we ask this of you? I promise we'll bring back Pete and Marco."

"Ohhh… I can't believe this!" Katie was on the verge of tears.

Chela swooped in and hugged her. "Please, Katie," she urged, her voice shaking, "do as we tell you. We absolutely cannot take you with us. You're too willing to sacrifice yourself…"

Oliver was in complete agreement. They tried their best to console their sniffling friend. Meanwhile, Miligan spun around.

"That's settled, then. Let's meet back here in two hours. Catch up Ms. Hibiya for me, will you? And come prepared."

With that, the Snake-Eyed Witch left. Oliver shot Chela a look over Katie's head, and she nodded.

Chela and Katie exited the academy, returned to the girls' dorm, and headed straight for their room. When they arrived, Chela gently knocked on the door.

"…It's me. May I come in, Nanao?"

"Mm, enter."

The reply was immediate. Chela and Katie slowly opened the door and stepped into the room—and stared in shock. Nanao was sitting on her knees waiting for them, bags packed and ready for a descent into the labyrinth.

"'Tis time to go, then?"

Her eyes fluttered open. Chela and Katie were taken aback.

"You're already packed…?"

"I knew your hearts were set the moment this all began. I have simply been awaiting your summons."

Nanao got down from the bed and stood before them.

Chela had prepared a whole speech that was no longer needed—but the lack of a preamble lent a graver tone to her next question. "Like I said earlier, we should expect the worst. Are you still prepared to go?"

She had to ask. At breakfast, Nanao had pointed out that there was no proof Pete was still alive. Risking their lives to venture down into the labyrinth and save him could be a waste of time—or worse, the rescuers would need rescuing.

The Azian girl nodded without hesitation. A terribly serene smile was on her lips.

"No matter the result, 'tis the same—whether we go to rescue a friend or retrieve a corpse."

Chela's and Katie's chests tightened. On the battlefields Nanao had survived prior to joining the academy, this must have been par for the course.

"…I'm sorry, Nanao… I can't go…"

Katie apologized with tears in her eyes, then squeezed Nanao's arm. Chela explained Miligan's plan, and Nanao nodded and smiled.

"You and Guy shall be holding down the fort, then. I entrust you two with our studies."

"…Yeah, leave it to us. You'll get the best notes you've ever read!"

Katie wiped her tears, promised to do her very best, and embraced her friend tightly. They would definitely meet again. Her battle was to wait and believe in them.

"…I can't come, too?"

Meanwhile, in the boys' dorm, Oliver explained the situation to Guy.

Upon realizing no amount of begging would allow him to help search for Pete, Guy slumped his shoulders and heaved a great sigh.

"…I hate saying it, but I can't deny I'd hold you back."

"Guy…"

"Here…take this."

Guy retrieved something from on top of his bed and handed it to Oliver: a number of thick, round, wrapped objects and a few drawstring pouches packed full to bursting. He explained their contents as Oliver took them from him.

"Those are my best rations, plus some bundles of toolplant seeds I raised and harvested. They're how I instantly made that barricade the other day. I'm guessing you already know how to use 'em."

"…Yeah, that barricade worked really well. I'll be sure to use these if I need to."

Oliver smiled and nodded, gratefully accepting his friend's assistance.

Guy continued, slightly muted. "The rations should taste much better than anything you can buy at the store… I mean, you gotta eat, right? Might as well have it taste good. Make sure to save one for Pete, too. Bet he's starving."

He stopped there, but after a while, the silence seemed too much for him, and he raked his hands through his hair. Oliver understood his pain all too well. If their positions were reversed, he'd likely feel the exact same way.

"Ahhh, damn it! I hate gettin' told I hafta stay behind. It's pathetic… Listen, don't do anything crazy. I'm being serious here!"

His voice cracked as he grabbed Oliver by the shoulders. His fingers squeezed painfully, but Oliver only nodded confidently.

"I swear to you we'll all come back alive—including Pete."

He promised to survive so that he could see this kindhearted friend of his again.

Later, at the time and hall designated by Miligan, Oliver and Guy arrived to find a bunch of familiar faces.

"We're all here, then. Not said your good-byes yet?" Miligan asked as she grinned at Guy and Katie, who were not part of the rescue team. "Doesn't matter to me, but do it silently at least. With the academy in a state of emergency, second-years and below aren't allowed into the labyrinth. If the prefects catch us, there'll be hell to pay."

And with that warning, the witch turned on her heel and strode down the hall. The five of them followed after her. Moving quietly and cautiously, they ascended to the second floor, hiding whenever an older student was coming. It took them ten minutes to reach their destination classroom. On the wall was a painting of a night sky; Miligan stopped right in front of it.

"This will be our entrance tonight. It's possible we could be attacked as soon as we enter, so I'll go first. Oh, but before that..."

She turned around suddenly, produced something from her robe pocket, and handed it to Katie.

"Katie, take care of Milihand. Think of her as my will and testament."

"...Huh?"

Katie instinctively accepted the object but froze the moment she looked at the thing she was holding—a severed hand. Miligan's left hand to be precise, severed by Nanao and residence of the basilisk eye: In a dark twist, Miligan had given it artificial life and turned it into her familiar. The basilisk eye in the center of its palm stared up at Katie. It seemed almost friendly.

"If I don't make it back here alive, she'll serve as the key to reading my research results. She can be needy, so be kind to her."

"Wh-what...? H-hold on a second!"

Milihand scuttled up Katie's arm to her shoulder and, determining this as its spot, "sat" down. Oliver sighed. The disembodied hand seemed to have the same affection for Katie as its master.

"Thanks. Bye!"

"Wait—!"

Miligan slipped into the painting despite Katie's confusion. Now it was their turn. Katie struggled to find the right words, so Chela and Oliver smiled at her reassuringly.

"It'll be fine, Katie," said Chela. "I won't let anyone die."

"Neither will I. All ready, Nanao?"

His mind set, Oliver turned to the girl beside him for one final confirmation.

Nanao nodded without the slightest hesitation. "I was born ready. Now—to battle!"

On her signal, the three of them jumped into the painting.

"......"

"......"

Even after they were gone and the dark classroom had gone silent, Guy and Katie continued to stare at the painting for quite a while.

CHAPTER 2

The Bustling Forest

The arts of magic are passed down from generation to generation. Thus, their machinations are inevitably tied to the ideas and secrets of the family that stewards them. From parent to child and so on—mage family lines may branch but are never broken. While it is not as simple as saying "the older, the better" in regards to family lines, houses with longer histories command a fair amount of respect and fear. That history represents years of refinement—countless successes and failures. A staggeringly large amount of trial and error over a similarly vast amount of time results in these houses' characteristic abilities.

The Salvadori family is one of these mage houses, with a distinguished history not seen in many others. Its beginnings can be traced back to even before the establishment of the Great Calendar, when the relationship between humans and demi-humans wasn't as strained. As if proof of this, pure-blooded succubi—the progenitor of the Salvadori line—are now considered extinct.

"A great number of creatures' seeds are going to mix together in here—like something cooking in a cauldron."

She stroked her abdomen with a white fingertip. Ophelia spoke of the destiny her family had bestowed upon her. On the other side of the table, listening to her speech, sat a slightly older teen—Carlos Whitrow.

"Apparently, succubi were originally extremely amenable to mating with other species," Ophelia continued. "If anything caught their fancy, they'd seduce in their target, forcibly extract their seed, and pass on the unique properties to their children. This was the survival strategy they chose."

Her voice was steady, but Carlos could sense her searching their expression. Her words were clearly meant to incite a reaction for her to judge.

"But if you ask whether this was the correct decision, then it seems it wasn't. All that lovely seed died along with the succubi when they went extinct. My mother claimed they confused their methods with their goals. At some point, the succubi needed to decide on a clear direction. Ironic, considering seeking direction is exactly why they spread their legs for every able-bodied male... Heh."

The sound of her own chuckling interrupted her. It pained Carlos to see her laughing so heartily at her own flesh and blood. What terrible orders had she accepted without complaint from her family that led her to such pitiful self-derision?

"Funny, isn't it? They got so full of themselves, snagging every man in sight, only to end up dying as harlots no one would dare get involved with."

"......"

Carlos searched for the right words but was unable to find them. There were many things they'd like to say. They'd love to tell her *that's not true* until their voice gave out. But no matter what they said now, they knew it would fall on deaf ears. Ophelia cocked her head quizzically as Carlos suffered in silence. Slight hesitation appeared on her face, as if surprised by this reaction, but she soon wiped it away and continued speaking.

"And yet—wouldn't our ancestors be shocked to see us Salvadoris now?"

Her lips cracked into a smile, and she scanned her surroundings. Strange groans filled the dim room as countless grotesque creatures crawled about.

"......"

Carlos could never allow so much as a grimace to surface on their face. That was the rule they'd decided on upon being shown to this room—for some of the twisted creatures residing here had been birthed by Ophelia herself.

"Or would they berate us, I wonder, for giving birth countless times not in search of a new hybrid, rather than for survival? Would it disgust them to see their descendants, looking like so much genetic tossed salad...?"

*

Slowly, ever so slowly, his consciousness rose out of the sweet honeypot.

"Ungh..."

It was hard to breathe; he hated waking with every fiber of his being. His whole body felt sluggish as it rejected moving even a single finger, yet so unpleasant that he couldn't stay asleep even a second longer.

"......Hah...ah...!"

Pete thrust his hands against the disgustingly warm floor and slowly lifted himself up. His vision was blurry. He instinctively raised a hand to his face to find his glasses were gone. Panicking, he searched his robe and fortunately found his spare. Putting them on made his vision clearer, but at the same time, the overwhelming intensity of the sight before him devastated his mind.

"—?!"

The floor beneath his hand was pulsating strangely, and the unique elasticity of living flesh pushed back against his palm. The walls were of similar construction, while in front was what appeared to be iron bars—on closer inspection, these actually grew out of the floor.

A prison of flesh. That was the only way to describe this place.

"...Wh-where am I...?"

As the fog in his mind cleared, his memories slowly returned. He recalled descending into the labyrinth with his friends, watching the duel between them and their classmates, being completely enthralled by Oliver's seemingly endless bag of sword tricks—and the appearance of those magical beasts the moment the duel was finished, disrupting their brief respite.

"Did everyone get captured…?"

He looked around the cell and saw a large number of students in the exact same situation. There were over ten of them, mostly first- and second-years. From their snoring, he could tell they were alive, but none seemed close to waking. He realized that must have been him a few moments ago. He reached out cautiously toward one to try and wake them when all of a sudden, he heard footsteps.

"…!"

He dropped to the floor and tried his hardest to feign sleep. There was no deep reasoning behind it. It simply seemed, on an instinctual level, that being the only one awake was dangerous.

The footsteps from outside the cell soon approached him. He could feel someone—or something—staring down at him, but he was too scared to even try and catch a peek. He funneled all his efforts into appearing unconscious when he heard a whisper:

"…All sound asleep. Be good little boys now and stay that way. If you never wake, it'll all just be a bad dream."

Pete nearly screamed, but he somehow managed to contain himself. He could never forget that voice. It belonged to an older student he'd met during the academy's "encroachment" phase with Oliver and Chela that night not long after the entrance ceremony.

"……"

After a while, the person's footsteps faded into the distance. But Pete remained still for a long time before carefully getting up. One wrong move and he was dead. He might not understand the situation he was in, but his instincts understood this at least.

Suppressing the urge to fall into despair, he desperately thought— how could he increase his chances of survival? What actions would allow him to return to the surface alive?

✳

The labyrinth's first layer was unusually empty. They'd walked for over an hour along the path but run into no other students. President Godfrey's imposition of martial law seemed to be effective.

"......"

For Oliver, the silence reinforced how abnormal the present situation was, if even a place as dangerous as Kimberly could end up like this.

"Let me tell you a few things while I still have the chance."

Miligan, their lead on this rescue mission, suddenly broke the silence. The three friends listened intently to the witch's next words.

"First, Ophelia Salvadori outclasses me. Even a conservative estimate would put her at double my ability. Consider it a guaranteed loss if we go at her head-on."

This first fact alone was enough to chill Oliver's spine. Their near-deadly battle with the Snake-Eyed Witch was still fresh in his memory. They'd nabbed victory by a hairbreadth, but it was clear that Miligan had been toying with them the entire time. She was much more powerful, and if she'd used her full strength, Oliver and his friends would have never stood a chance. And now this fearsome witch was telling them she was guaranteed to lose to Ophelia Salvadori.

"Thus, what we should be thinking about is how we can rescue Pete without being discovered. Everyone fine with that?"

"...No objections here," Chela replied. "Do you have any idea where Pete's being held?"

"In her workshop. I'm almost certain of it. I've also got a good idea of what she's going to use him for, too."

"What's happened to our friend?!" Chela cried.

Miligan put a hand to her chin pensively. "I suspect she's draining him of his vitality. She won't be going for his sperm itself but the mana attributed to his male sex. Ophelia requires this for her rituals. Normally she'd obtain it through intercourse, but in this case, she's after so much of it that she kidnapped a bunch of younger students to speed up the process."

"...Does this 'process' involve pain?" Chela asked.

"Nope. She'll put her captives to sleep in order to keep them from struggling, so it shouldn't be especially painful. They might experience some nightmares, though," the witch stated quite matter-of-factly, although that was due more to indifference than any attempt to console Chela.

Oliver frowned. This line of thinking had to be more of a fourth-year thing.

"However, every day that passes makes the captives weaker. Obviously, since their vitality's being drained. Whether she plans to drain Pete completely, however, I can't say for sure. You'd have to ask her yourself."

Miligan went quiet again.

Suddenly, Chela's expression changed.

"Hold on... She's extracting his *male* mana?" the ringleted girl repeated back, then looked at Oliver next to her. He nodded in understanding. "Oliver...!"

"Yeah...this could be bad."

"...Hmm? What are we panicking about?" Confused, Miligan cocked her head.

Oliver debated whether or not to explain, but Nanao beat him to the punch.

"Pete recently awakened as a reversi."

"Nanao?!"

He stared at her in disbelief, but Nanao quietly shook her head. "If we are to be partners on this expedition, then it is not something we should hide. Our past quarrels aside—are we not all brothers and sisters in this quest into the depths of hell?"

She looked at him so earnestly that the words died in Oliver's throat. Her ability to accept people as enemies or allies at a moment's notice was astounding, most likely another quality forged on the battlefield.

Finally grasping the situation, the Snake-Eyed Witch grinned. "Yes, it would be helpful if we could not keep any secrets. So...a reversi. That's quite a rare phenomenon. And with such...perfect timing, too."

Oliver and Chela were in total agreement here. It was a catastrophic mismatch. Pete's sex could change between male and female almost daily, ruining any chance Ophelia had of peacefully extracting the male mana she so desired.

"Unfortunately, that's just another reason we need to hurry. Normally, that would make him a rare specimen, giving reason to extend his life. But with Ophelia consumed by the spell, she'll only see a reversi as a hindrance to her ritual. If she finds out, his life will definitely be on a shorter clock."

"All the more reason to make haste!" Chela's pace quickened with panic.

However, Miligan gently placed a hand on her shoulder. "Not too much haste, Ms. McFarlane. Ophelia's workshop is somewhere on the third layer. You haven't forgotten, have you? In order to get there, we must first traverse the *second* layer."

Her tone was ice-cold, and Chela stopped in her tracks. Oliver nodded heavily, too. She was right. Speed was not the highest priority; first, they needed to figure out how to reach Pete alive.

"Go out there unprepared and you'll wind up dead in an instant. You three have only experienced the entrance to the labyrinth. I promise we'll go as quickly as possible, so just listen to your elder's advice, okay?"

"...Understood. Forgive me. I lost my cool." Mollified, Chela apologized.

Miligan smiled and returned her gaze to the path ahead. "Good girl. And look, we're almost to your secret base."

Without realizing it, they'd set foot on familiar ground. They headed for the door hidden in the wall, spoke the password, and entered the workshop in which the six friends had once spent the night. The party of four passed through the empty living room into the spacious common room next door.

"Marco...! You're okay!"

The moment they opened the door, they spotted a large figure curled up in the corner; Oliver couldn't help crying out his name.

Marco stirred from his slumber, raising his head.

"Unh—Oliver. I okay. Where Katie?"

"She's okay, too! I'm sorry for leaving you behind!"

Marco's first thoughts were for Katie's safety, so Oliver ran over and brought him up to speed. Miligan, entering the room behind them, let out a low whistle.

"Well, isn't this a good omen. Marco, did the chimera not go after you?"

"Unh. They no chase me," Marco responded as he backed up against the wall. He watched her with fear and alarm; it was no wonder, considering what she'd done to him. Miligan, however, didn't seem to care about this at all and nodded.

"That backs up my hypothesis," Miligan said. "The chimeras weren't going berserk—they were acting on Ophelia's orders. She's still capable of some reason, at least for now."

Chela's expression brightened a tiny bit. Although it provided only a temporary peace of mind, this was the first bit of good news they'd received so far.

"Even if she discovers he's a reversi, Ophelia has no reason to actively try to kill Pete. He's a first-year—hardly anyone she needs to worry about. If she still has her wits about her, she can simply put him to sleep. If she kills him, it will mean that she's on the verge of losing it entirely."

"…So we have a little bit of time?"

"By my best guess, yeah. This is just based on my experience going to school with her for the past four years, but Ophelia has amazing self-control. Even if she is on the brink of being consumed by the spell, she won't lose her mind so easily. I have faith in that."

Miligan stated this quite plainly. Ophelia Salvadori was just a monstrous older student to the three friends, but to Miligan, she was a classmate of four years. You pick up on a few things over such a long period of time.

"The first-years I'm more worried about are you three. Even with my help, I don't know if you can make it to the third layer in one piece."

Miligan's expression was oddly serious. She returned to the living room and began picking up supplies. The three first-years took her cue to resume their advance; they couldn't afford to sit back and relax here. They hurriedly portioned out some rations for Marco to eat.

"We'll come back for you in a few days," said Oliver. "I'm sorry, Marco, but please stay inside the workshop until then. We don't know what kind of danger lies outside."

"Okay. Oliver, Nanao, Chela...be safe."

He gave each of them a big handshake. Promising to meet again soon, the three of them left the secret base with Miligan. One day, the Sword Roses would be reunited.

"Mm?"

They began walking through the labyrinth, and as they approached the entrance to the second layer, Miligan sensed something and stopped. Oliver and the girls noticed it a second later—the presence of something strange from within the depths of the path ahead. Whatever it was, it was larger than any human and was blocking their way.

"Our first hurdle. So this is the thing that had you all running for your lives?"

"...!"

They proceeded ahead, athames drawn and ready, until they finally saw it: a giant mass over twenty feet high and densely covered in wriggling tentacles. Chela swallowed audibly. There was no way to tell if it was the exact same one from that night, but it was definitely a chimera like the one that had abducted Albright, Willock, and Pete before their very eyes.

Miligan strode forward, not bothering to stay out of sight, and the chimera quickly took notice of their party. The Snake-Eyed Witch squared off with the beast from about fifteen yards apart.

"You made the right choice, retreating," said Miligan. "If you'd tried to take on one of Ophelia's chimera without a plan, you'd all be her captives right now, too. You'd have to be at least a third-year in order to take down one of these."

The witch approved of their decision. Oliver and Chela recalled the moment Pete was kidnapped, and their hearts ached in union. That night, they had been powerless against this magical beast.

"But if we don't push through this monster, we can't save Pete. This won't be easy. So what do you think we should do?" Miligan asked as she took a step forward. Not a shred of fear or hesitation emanated from her as she faced down the beast. "The answer's simple—watch and learn."

She leaped toward the beast, its tentacles rushing to meet her. Oliver swallowed. How was she planning on dealing with that many tentacles at close range?

"Deformatio!"

She chanted a spell, and rays of light burst from her athame, striking the ground in multiple places. Instantly, the stone floor rose up, as if being shaped by an invisible hand; the result was a wobbling lump of stone about the size of a human. Its center of gravity was low, allowing it to tilt but never topple over—a roly-poly toy.

"Lesson one: These things are practically blind!"

As Miligan shouted, a tentacle shot out and grabbed the decoy. The first-years gawked—the roly-poly was actually throwing the beast off. Miligan ignored their shock and continued.

"Those tentacles are just like bangs: They make it hard to see—okay, I'm kidding. The simple answer is, it's not capable of both seeing well *and* controlling all those tentacles. It's something you'll learn eventually in magical biology: The nervous system has its limits," she explained with unwavering conviction. "Deformatio!"

The newly formed decoys differed in size and shape; she was gauging the beast's reaction.

"So if it's not using vision, then what sense is it using to try and capture us? Touch is out of the question, since it would have to come in contact with us first. So let's test its hearing and thermal detection. In other words, vibrations and heat—all I have to do is disturb these elements with any old spell. Flammumna!"

She added another spell—a practical application of a fire spell in pillar form. It continued to burn in the location it was cast and mixed together with the other decoys; the floor surrounding Miligan burned red. The tentacles began writhing even more chaotically.

"Bingo. So seventy percent vibration, thirty percent heat. And about ninety percent of how it assesses the outside world is with the sensory organs in the tentacles covering its body. It can sense mana, too, of course, but it doesn't have the accuracy to extrapolate a moving human's location. We can ignore it."

Completely overwhelmed by the multiple decoys and flame pillars, the beast's tentacles failed to find its prey. This seemed to support Miligan's claims. If it had good eyesight, it wouldn't be struggling so hard to distinguish between the decoys and the humans.

"Lesson two: The golden rule of facing large magical beasts is to never stand in front of them. If it attacked with all its tentacles at once, even I wouldn't be able to defend myself. So keep moving. Don't stop for even a second; scatter your opponent's focus. This is where magical decoys are really useful!"

Miligan continued flitting about, never stopping. Oliver kept his eyes as wide as possible, so as not to miss a single moment. Her phantasmagoric footwork, a combination of control over her center of gravity and territory magic, must have made her seem like mist to the poor-sighted beast.

"One or two tentacles are no threat. In fact, those attacks are your chance to counter and weaken your opponent. You must never rush the battle—a larger magical beast's stamina is fundamentally different from ours. Get your hits in where you can, and only go for the kill once it's significantly weakened. **Impetus!**"

She weaved in a spell among her risky dodging, carving out a chunk from the chimera's body. With its tentacles distracted by her multiple decoys, its main body was wide open. The giant creature, which had withstood even Chela's double incantation when protected by its tentacles, winced as Miligan's wind blade sliced into it.

"That said, we don't have unlimited time. A louder fight will draw the attention of other beasts, if this thing's not already summoning its friends. The tides might turn if another one shows up. So lesson three: Don't fight recklessly. Envision the steps you need to take to deal the final blow, then steadily execute your plan."

With every lesson she imparted, the battle progressed slowly but surely. Just a few more weakening strikes and she'd be ready to go for the kill—or so Oliver and the girls thought, but suddenly the beast made an unexpected move. The tentacles distracted by the decoys regrouped, then shot through the air toward Miligan. The witch jumped to the side and dodged, her lips curled in a smile.

"It's started learning. This is what's annoying about Ophelia's chimeras: They aren't stupid. If you use the same strategy long enough, they'll adapt. It's learning to tell the difference between my decoys and me. Time to turn the tables!"

And with that announcement, Miligan switched tactics. She began walking straight toward the beast without any tricks, as if her quick and complicated movements from before were just an illusion. She was practically strolling toward the creature; Oliver's jaw dropped to the floor.

But it didn't matter. The beast didn't react in the slightest to her suicidal plan. Its tentacles wandered about, as if it had once again lost sight of the prey it had previously locked on to.

"Sorry, you're finished. **Tonitrus!**"

Miligan walked right up to the beast's face and ruthlessly stabbed her athame into its exposed cranium. Simultaneously, she chanted a spell—electricity ripped through its internal organs and fried its brain. The beast convulsed, then collapsed without even a scream.

"It knew the simple movements were my decoys, and the complicated movements were me—so I turned the concept on its head."

The Snake-Eyed Witch gazed down at the beast's corpse, not a hair out of place. It was an incredibly dramatic end to the battle, far beyond anything Oliver had imagined.

"You made it look so easy...," Chela muttered to herself.

Miligan spun around to face them again and grinned. "You see now, Ms. McFarlane? The fact that the tentacles covering it were resistant to electricity made it clear that its inner body was weak to electricity. Once you've determined your opponent's weak point, even a single incantation is more than enough. As long as you determine the beast's origin, that will naturally narrow down the locations of its brain and heart."

She pointed at the giant corpse behind her. Oliver agreed. He'd had a feeling this chimera was based on a type of wingless landwyrm. One could add organs such as tentacles after the fact, but the brain and spinal cord—the species' most fundamental parts—were not so easily modified.

"Easier said than done, of course," Miligan continued. "Ideally, you'd break the process down into separate steps: observing the ecology, determining the weak point, and building a strategy. If the beast has already been documented, the first two steps can be achieved through studying the corresponding literature. Ophelia's chimeras, however, are basically each a new species, which complicates things." Miligan shrugged.

She was completely right. When they'd faced the chimeras, it was their first time seeing them, and they were overwhelmed. But now that she had broken down the facts, these chimeras were certainly not in any way superior to the garuda. All the more reason why knowing your enemy was imperative.

"I won't tell you to replicate on your own what I did. Instead, I want you three to learn to do it together. That's my minimum requirement before I take you to the third layer."

""—!""

"If you can't complete this assignment before we exit the second layer, well, I'm sorry, but your adventure ends there. Don't worry—I'll escort you back to the surface," the witch gently assured them.

Repeat what she just did by the time they left the second layer? Oliver and Chela were visibly anxious at such a heavy assignment. The Azian girl spoke up, unperturbed.

"Then I shall take the third step."

"Nanao?"

"We can do it, Oliver. Recall our battle with the garuda."

Nanao smiled at him encouragingly. Oliver thought back to that night—although he'd had some previous knowledge, the garuda was indeed something he'd never faced before.

"That's right—you're garuda slayers," said Miligan. "I may have weakened it, but that was a full-blown divine beast underling. I wouldn't have brought you here otherwise. What about you, Ms. McFarlane? Think you have what it takes to do the same?"

Miligan turned back to face Chela, who nodded vigorously as if to shake off her worries.

"Your lesson was so detailed. It would be impossible to say no." Her usual dignity regained, Chela rounded on the Azian girl. "And, Nanao! Quit throwing yourself into danger. The three of us will do it all together—observation, determining weakness, and building a strategy."

"Mm, is that so? ...Very well. I shall try to make use of my brain."

Nanao crossed her arms as she struggled to get the gears turning.

Oliver grinned. It would seem she'd chosen the dangerous job not out of a sense of duty but simply to avoid a role that required thinking.

"...We'll definitely master it. Will you teach us, Ms. Miligan?" Oliver asked, bolstered by the girls' confidence. The corners of Miligan's lips curved upward into a smirk.

"Sure. This is *exactly* why I can't get enough of mentoring younger students!" Miligan then turned her gaze to the magical beast's corpse. "From here on, we'll be entering the second layer, the bustling forest. Even without Ophelia's chimeras crawling around, it's plenty dangerous—enough to be called a first-years' graveyard. I'll teach you all step-by-step. Oliver, Nanao, Chela, don't dawdle—come with me."

""""Yes, ma'am!"""""

There was a friendlier tone to her voice, and the three of them didn't reject it. Of course, they couldn't just forget past events. But right now, she was an invaluable teacher who would show them how to survive in the labyrinth. They swore not to miss a single word the Snake-Eyed Witch spoke as they followed her to the next layer.

At the same time, on the second layer that the party was about to step into, in a corner of the bustling forest, thick with green trees and home to countless magical creatures...

"Ignis!"

"GYAAAAAAAAAAHHHH!"

A torrent of flames wrapped around the chimera. The waves of hot wind billowing outward spoke volumes of the intense heat it generated. It must not have dodged the single-incantation spell because of its confidence in its tough body. This was certainly not a mistake. The scale armor that covered its body should have deflected most spells—if they hadn't been cast by this young man.

"AAH... AAH..."

Not even its dying howls lasted very long. Surrounded by incredible heat, its body quickly turned to ash. Petty things like "natural resistance" posed no trouble for the flames. When it came to pure magical output, any attempt to measure Alvin Godfrey on a normal scale was a grave error. Carlos Whitrow was reminded of this as they watched the battle.

"All the chimeras we've run into so far have been new breeds... Can't let our guards down for even a second." Godfrey sheathed his athame and sighed. The prefects had split into pairs after entering the labyrinth. So far, Carlos and Godfrey had encountered and killed six chimeras on their journey.

"I'd expect as much when Lia gets serious," said Carlos. "It's a scary experience for anyone to fight an unknown magical beast. Especially if you're trying to conserve mana. Makes us seem like Gnostic Hunters."

Sorrow colored their androgynous features. There was no one at Kimberly who knew the one behind all this trouble better than Carlos. Godfrey strode away from the chimera's ashes, a troubled expression on his face. "In that case, I should be grateful to her. She's providing me with valuable field experience."

"Oh? Have you already decided what you'll do after graduation? Seems just yesterday you were still conflicted."

"Nothing's set in stone. But ultimately, fighting's the only thing I'm any good at. So as long as I'm fighting to protect someone, I can imagine myself doing the same thing even when I leave the academy," Godfrey replied with a sigh. After five years at Kimberly, he'd learned all too well what he was and wasn't capable of, as well as what sort of person he ought to be in this world. Considering their friend's feelings and potential future, Carlos's expression clouded.

"The Gnostic Hunters' hellscape is nothing like Kimberly's," said Carlos. "And there's no guarantee that you'll find kindred spirits like you did here... Will you manage?"

"I don't know... But if you came with me, it'd make things a lot easier."

Godfrey muttered his true feelings under his breath; a second later, he realized his mistake and shut his mouth in embarrassment.

A kind smile appeared on his old friend's face. "I'm sorry I can't go with you... Maybe my worries are unfounded, though. There are lots of other people out there who would follow you anywhere," said Carlos.

"That's nice to hear, but whether I can trust them to have my back is another matter. I don't want to bring anyone likely to die right away onto the battlefield."

Godfrey's expression was tinged with gloom. It was true that he had many allies currently. Any number of them would accompany him to the grave without hesitation if he asked. But that made it all that much harder to ask. Carlos, who understood his conflict better than anyone, nodded. "And that's exactly why I think the Gnostic Hunters would want you so badly."

"...I'm not so sure. I have a feeling there are plenty of sixth- and seventh-years even stronger than I am."

"Even so, the fact of the matter is every student at the academy fears you. That includes the sixth- and seventh-year monsters."

They stated the absolute truth matter-of-factly. But despite their valuation, something bitter rose in Godfrey's face.

"I'd rather be loved than feared. Especially by my juniors."

"They're not mutually exclusive. Of course, I don't fear you, Al."

Carlos beamed from ear to ear; Godfrey pursed his lips and scratched the back of his head. Carlos always managed to get him with that face ever since they were first-years. The two of them continued to walk in silence for a bit, when Godfrey suddenly stopped.

"Hold on. Someone's coming."

They got into defensive stances. A few seconds later, the bushes in front of them shook, and someone crawled out from within—short in stature, covered in dirt and mud. Their school uniform was beyond recognition, but luckily their necktie color identified them as a sixth-year. Upon seeing Godfrey and Carlos, the sixth-year's face lit up.

"...Oh? Ohhh? Ohhhh? Today's my lucky day!"

"Mr. Walker?"

Godfrey was taken aback by the unexpected run-in. Kevin Walker, Kimberly Magic Academy sixth-year, aka the Survivor. He was the current president of the Labyrinth Gourmet Club and famous among the student body for returning alive after spending half a year in the labyrinth's depths.

"Man, what luck! I figured this route might be a winner if you two were taking it! Okay, sure, it was just a hunch. But the point is, I was waiting for someone to happen by so I could give them this! ...Oh, you guys hungry? I have a swamp shrimp I caught in the bog over there. Wanna have a barbecue?"

"P-please calm down," said Godfrey.

"You were waiting for us, Kevin?" Carlos asked.

"Hmm? Ah, right, I was. Here, I wanted to give you this."

Walker clapped his hands when he remembered his errand. He produced an old, worn notebook from his pocket and handed it to Carlos. They took it and scanned through it while Godfrey peered over their shoulder.

"This is…"

"A map of the third layer. I explored as much as I could and recorded it in there. The landscape's really changed recently, probably thanks to Lia's influence. Be careful. The place is crawling with chimeras like nothing I've ever seen," said Walker, as if he had seen the creatures himself.

Godfrey's jaw dropped, realizing he wasn't being figurative. What he was saying was…

"…You went down to the third layer all alone? While all this is going on?"

"Yup. But I've gotta apologize—I couldn't find her workshop. First-years were kidnapped this time around, so we need to hurry. This should help your rescue mission, so I'm sharing it with y— Oh?"

His rapid-fire speech was suddenly cut off. Carlos's long, slender arms wrapped tightly around the sixth-year's short frame. They didn't seem bothered in the least by the mud and filth.

"Thank you, Kevin. Thank you…"

"Carlos…"

Godfrey was as overcome with emotion as his friend. Neither of them was being dramatic, either. Past or present, there were very few older students who would lend a helping hand. After a few moments, Walker patted Carlos's shoulder.

"Ha-ha! What're you saying, Carlos? A senior helps out his juniors, even without being asked. You guys believe the same, don't you?" he said, as if it was the most natural thing in the world, showing his approval for their efforts.

Carlos smiled and let Walker go.

Walker spun around and said, "Anyway, I think I'll venture down again. I got the lay of the land last time, so I should be able to search deeper now."

"Wha—? W-wait a second. You could come with us!" said Godfrey.

"Mm, no thanks. I prefer going solo. You guys know that, right?"

He lightly waved good-bye and then shuffled into the bushes again. They tried to call out and stop him, but Walker was firm.

"I'll be fine. I'm not gonna die in the labyrinth. Anyway, later!"

And with that, the Survivor disappeared into the darkness. Godfrey stared after him for a bit, dumbfounded, and then sighed heavily.

"...He never changes."

"Nope. He's always been a huge help to us ever since we were first-years."

Carlos smiled and nodded.

Walker was something of a mentor—in the best way, with no ulterior motives to be found. As grateful as they were, Godfrey and Carlos refocused on the path ahead.

"Thanks to him, we're a lot closer to Lia now. Let's go, Al."

"Yeah. Let's hurry."

The two friends nodded to each other, then started off again. There was still a long way to go and not much time left.

After clearing their first hurdle and entering the second layer, they stepped into a landscape beyond Oliver's imagination.

"Take this fruit, for example. Looks delicious, right? However..."

As she lectured, the Snake-Eyed Witch reached out her left hand toward the stubby fruit tree. Suddenly, the fruit split open and snapped at her like a starving dog. Miligan quickly withdrew her hand, and the fruit tree caught only air, gnashing its teeth in search of prey.

"If you try to eat it, it'll eat you. Losing a finger to one of these is considered your second-layer baptism. It's one of the cuter traps out there, but if you lose your dominant hand, you won't be able to use your wand, and that's bad news. If you're going to touch something unknown, take the proper precautions. If nothing else, at least make a habit of starting with your nondominant hand."

Miligan launched into her second-layer lesson. Nanao studied the violent fruit tree, her brow furrowed.

"Mm. Then this is not edible?" she asked.

"Oh, it is. Just cast a spell to knock it out, then cut off the fruit. It's probably eaten a bunch of students' fingers, but if you're fine with that, go ahead."

"…Nanao, I'm not saying you can't eat anything down here, but let's at least find something less carnivorous."

Oliver had to pull her back as she stared intently at it, and the four of them resumed walking through the forest. The verdant greenery overpowered their noses; the shadows were teeming with life big and small. Oliver and the girls moved cautiously, and Miligan sucked in a hearty breath.

"Heh-heh-heh. This is fun. The second layer is my favorite place for a stroll. The ecosystem of plants and animals is so varied that there's always something interesting nearby. I wanna bring Katie here one day soon."

"Just a stroll, huh…?" Chela muttered, half in disbelief and half amazed. They couldn't bring themselves to relax like Miligan; there was no telling when they'd run into a threat.

Miligan chuckled at their nervousness. "Of course, now's a little different. We could run into one of Ophelia's chimeras at any time. Still, I'm comfortable enough that we can have a chat, if you like."

"…I see. Then would you mind if I test something?" Oliver suggested, seizing on the opportunity while there was no immediate danger.

Miligan drew closer, curious, and the boy decided it would be faster to show her than explain. First, he took a seed out of his drawstring pouch and tossed it on the ground. Next, he pulled out his wand and cast a growth-enhancing spell. It sprouted and flourished before his eyes, maturing into a young tree. It grew in a curve until the tip eventually pierced the ground again, forming an arch-shaped fence in front of them.

"Ooh, a toolplant? Look at how quickly it grew. And so strong, too. You've got some good seed there."

Miligan kicked at and shoved the completed fence in order to confirm her suspicions. Oliver nodded. "It's Guy's work. Should be useful in pinning down a magical beast during battle."

"Mr. Greenwood did this? …Hmm, not bad. I use toolplants a lot, but this is good enough to sell. They're quite at home in the second layer's soil, too."

"Heh, isn't he the best? Guy has quite the green thumb when it comes to magical flora," Chela boasted like a proud mother.

Miligan nodded, then turned back to Oliver. "Creativity is your greatest ally, so go ahead and experiment to your heart's content. I can cover for most of your fails."

"...Thanks," Oliver said shortly, then put the pouch of toolplant seeds back into his bag. Suddenly, he felt a pull at his sleeve.

"Oliver, I'm getting hungry."

Simultaneously, a loud growl came from Nanao's stomach. Oliver instinctively pinched his brow.

"That much is obvious... That growling's loud enough to attract a chimera. Ms. Miligan, I think it's time we ate."

"True, we've been hiking for about five hours. We've still got a long way to go, so let's take a breather."

Everyone agreed, and so the four of them set about finding a spot to eat. They happened upon a place surrounded by trees yet still fairly open; with magic, they cleared out the area a bit and created a rest stop. They finished it off with four impromptu chairs made from tool-plants, then sat down.

"Rest well, you three. In deep dives, breaks are as important as moving. And of course, you can't forget to get proper nutrition."

Miligan opened the bag on her lap and took out the rations. Oliver and the girls did the same and began eating. Opening their bundles from Guy, they discovered a long, dense cake—simple and rustic.

"It's a little early for this, but I'll tell you anyway—starting with this layer, setting up camp has a few rules. Don't go around just lighting fires, you hear me? That's the fastest way to attract magical beasts. There are a few points to keep in mind."

As they ate, Miligan lectured. Listening, Oliver cut his cake with his athame and popped a bite in his mouth. The extremely sweet sponge melted in his mouth but still maintained an enjoyable texture thanks to the walnuts and dried fruits. The strong sweetness was like a balm for his body after that long trek.

"Oliver, this is quite good."

"...Yeah. Very good."

"Truly delicious."

The three friends nodded in earnest. This seemed to pique Miligan's curiosity, so Chela traded her a bit of cake for a bite of her ration. The witch's eyes flew open the moment she bit into it.

"What is this? No fair, keeping such a treat a secret from me!"

As Miligan sang the cake's praises, Chela was as proud of her friend's success as if it were her own. Oliver watched the girls peacefully enjoying their meal—but his mind was focused elsewhere.

(...You're there, aren't you, Ms. Carste?)

He spoke not with his voice but with a micro-frequency of mana. He was careful to keep his output as low as possible, so as not to alert the others. But even if they did pick up on it, it would be impossible for them to recognize it as words without the predetermined cypher.

(...I am here. I would be by your side, but I cannot risk being noticed by Snake-Eye.)

Instantly, a reply came via the same method from behind—most likely from atop the trees. On the outside, Oliver appeared to be chatting pleasantly and resting, but underneath it all, he continued his conversation with Teresa Carste, master of invisibility.

(That's fine. Do you know how deep Brother and Sister are?)

(I met them on the first layer about eight hours ago. They must be ahead of us in the second layer by now. I have also spotted some of our allies and other older students.)

Oliver nodded mentally. He had no doubt that President Godfrey and a host of other upperclassmen were trying to contain the situation. It was reassuring to hear, but at the same time, running into any of them would prove problematic, considering they were first-years.

(I should tell you—I have been ordered to bring you back to the academy immediately upon locating you in the labyrinth.)

Oliver fell silent, then responded, trying to suss her out. (...Why aren't you doing that?)

(After the coronation, you became my liege in name and substance. It's only natural that I prioritize your desires over orders from Ms. Shannon and Mr. Gwyn.)

Teresa answered without hesitation, and Oliver was slightly taken aback by her position. She seemed quite serious about her role as his direct subordinate. Apparently, he needn't have worried about trying to turn her to his side.

(More importantly, Darius Grenville's substitute is bound to appear soon. Considering how troublesome those monsters will be, it serves no purpose to hesitate in facing someone like the Salvadori Harlot. In fact, this is a good chance to test our strength. Don't you agree, my liege?)

Her words struck Oliver's back harder than any whip. She was right— his true targets far outclassed Ophelia. Normal training methods were never going to make him their equal. In that sense, he ought to welcome this situation as an opportunity to grow stronger. It was good to reconfirm how reliable a subordinate Teresa was. So Oliver suggested a plan.

(Would your invisibility prove useful against Ophelia Salvadori's chimeras or against the witch herself?)

(From a certain distance, I can remain undetected without issue if I am alone. Should you require it, I can also act as a scout.)

(That'd be helpful. If you find anything dangerous in our path, let me know. But absolutely do not put yourself at risk.)

(Yes, my liege!)

Her reply was jubilant, and her innocence tugged at Oliver's heartstrings. He knew he was sending her on a suicide mission.

(Worry not, my liege. A lord should use his followers to their fullest effect. I am at your disposal.)

Teresa piped up, as if sensing his trepidation through the mana frequency. This made him feel guiltier, but Oliver swallowed his emotions and sent back a simple *(do it.)*

(There is…one other thing as well.)

Teresa offered a quiet addendum. The next moment, the frequency jumped in intensity despite her fine control over it earlier.

(I have always spoken in this manner. In a prior meeting, you suggested it might be forced. But it's not. I swear it!) Teresa stubbornly insisted, shouting so loudly that her voice practically rang in Oliver's ears. He was surprised, even more so when Nanao jumped up.

"? What is it, Nanao?"

"Someone is here."

She stared intently at the trees, her sharp senses apparently picking up on the ripples of mana. Oliver panicked but was also slightly relieved. A slipup like that was proof that Teresa was still a kid on the inside.

"Maybe we're being watched by a magical beast. It's not wise to stay in one spot for too long. We should move on, Ms. Miligan," Oliver commented, trying to create a diversion. He then got to his feet.

"Good idea," Miligan said with a nod. "Let's keep going."

They walked for another two hours through the forest before stumbling upon a completely different sight.

"Now, this is a bit of a predicament."

"Wow..."

Oliver couldn't immediately identify what he was looking up at—it was an extremely large tree. It was impossible to tell where the trunk ended and the branches began or even what was a root. It all wrapped and twisted together, with some limbs stretching into the air and sprouting leaves while others stuck into the ground, supporting the main body. Even at its thinnest point, the tree easily reached a diameter of ten yards.

"This is an irminsul, the gateway to the second layer of the labyrinth. In the surface world, it's a critically endangered species. Take a good look."

Miligan stroked the nearby bark as she explained.

"It's said that these trees will only sprout atop behemoth corpses. In ancient times, the earth was covered in these things—it's fascinating to think about. Oh, and here's our welcome party."

She looked up. Creatures with bony wings, long tails, and large beaks circled above the four of them, their shrill cries echoing endlessly.

"Those are small bird wyverns. Smart little rascals—they change their hunting patterns based on their prey. They'll wait for stronger prey to die, then scavenge the remains. But if the creature looks weak, the flock will attack as one. They eat everything, even bones, which is why they're nicknamed 'irminsul janitors.' Instructor Hedges wants a sky burial, right? He should ask these things to eat him," Miligan joked, then stepped on a giant branch and began walking atop it. Oliver and the girls followed her lead. The branch was like a road, cutting and snaking through the sky. The group proceeded cautiously as the wyverns above kept a close eye on them.

"...Are they going to be watching us until we get past this tree?" Chela asked.

"Probably. But it's not all bad news. Their flight pattern will change if a large magical beast is nearby. Just think of them as watchdogs."

Miligan seemed unfazed, but Oliver and the girls had never been here before, and they consequently couldn't be nearly as bold. The wyverns above them took a lot of their attention, but they could also sense countless presences hiding above the tangled branches. There was no telling where an attack could come from.

"There is technically a detour around this tree. And it's a bit safer, too. But it'd take a whole day to—"

"Then we go this way."

"Yes, every second is precious."

Nanao and Chela instantly replied.

Oliver nodded as well, looking at Miligan ahead of them.

"Guess I needn't have brought it up," she said. "All right, let's climb. Follow me!"

And so they began what was more like ascending a mountain than a tree. Keeping their eyes on their destination, they climbed from branch to branch. When the next branch was either too far or too high, they used their brooms, but Miligan insisted that they walk the majority of the time. According to her, attempting to ease the journey and fly when they didn't understand the geography or ecosystem was a recipe for disaster.

"'Tis quite a rough path, I must say."

"You can try to clean it up, but it'll be overgrown in no time. Careful not to trip."

"…I should have asked earlier, but how is there a sun here?" Chela said, peering up at the rays of light shining down from above as they ascended the steep branches.

Miligan answered as she cleared ivy from the path ahead. "It's a pre-Great Calendar legacy. Basically impossible to replicate the spell nowadays. Same goes for this labyrinth, really. That said, it's been nearly fully analyzed, and we now know that the source of its mana is on a deeper layer. Not even I know what the source is, though."

Oliver squinted and looked up at the artificial sun as he listened. A lot of magical techniques had been lost over time, and re-creating them was a great headache for modern-day mages. It was for this reason that reverse engineering was such a revered part of magical engineering. It was important they retrieved that ancient knowledge.

"Unlike on the surface, that sun never sets. And for plants, which don't need to sleep, this place is a paradise. It even rains periodically."

"…So it's a biotope? I can only imagine this environment was created by humans for the pursuit of magical biology studies," said Chela.

"If you want to know that, you'll have to study labyrinthology. As for the reason the labyrinth was created, well, we still don't have a clear answer to that," Miligan explained.

The conversation died off as the four of them hurried on. The path never leveled out, and the extreme hills and valleys sapped their strength.

"Hup…!"

It was the right decision not to bring Katie and Guy, Oliver thought as he cast Grave Step to create a foothold in order to jump to the next branch. Getting through this terrain required a certain level of footwork, and currently, even with a guide, those two would never have been able to keep up.

"…Hmm. They've gotten pretty close," Miligan muttered, slowing down. Oliver, taken aback, scanned their surroundings and saw countless eyes glittering behind every possible branch. Chela swallowed audibly. He'd sensed their presence but had no idea they'd grown in number.

"Ms. Miligan…"

"Don't draw. You'll agitate them. Just be ready to draw at a moment's notice," Miligan replied evenly, urging her juniors to remain calm. "A party of four has a fifty percent chance of passing through here without incident. It depends on how hungry these things are. And if it's mating season, they could attack without provocation. Luckily for us, they don't seem to be that on edge today."

"…They won't rely on numbers to attack, then?" Chela asked.

"It's happened in the past, and it turned out badly for them. They're scared of mages. And they have no way of knowing that three of us are only first-years."

Miligan's aim was to ease Chela's concerns, but Oliver's blood ran cold. That meant it was highly unusual for three first-years to be this far down in the labyrinth.

"The same can't be said for what's up ahead, though. Here comes the boss."

Miligan stopped. Her eyes were focused on a section of tree where dozens of branches much like the ones they'd traversed twisted and fused together, forming a large island in the shape of a basin. The "ground" was covered in thick soil, as if a pile of fallen leaves had been turned into mulch. And in the center of the island was a nest made from branches the size of trees. From within that nest, a massive shadow emerged, shaking the trees with every step it took.

"—!"

"…?!"

"Hoh."

"Stand your ground. Look straight at it. Don't show any fear. This is the boss of the irminsul's western face."

Miligan squared off against the approaching giant ape. It was easily three to five times their size, towering at over fifteen feet tall. Its entire body was covered with black fur, save for its face; its arms were slender and long compared to its legs and torso; it seemed capable of walking on two feet, but at present, it approached them on all fours. Oliver knew of many species of demon apes that lived in trees, but none that was this large. Perhaps it was a species unique to irminsuls.

"What's the matter, West? Why so on edge? You were never the type to bother with groups of people passing by," Miligan asked the beast calmly as she analyzed it from head to toe. It was missing patches of fur all over and had suffered a number of lacerations in its hide, reddish-black muscle peeking out from within. Upon more careful inspection, it was harder *not* to find a section of its body that wasn't wounded. It was even missing two whole fingers on its right hand.

"...Injured, huh? I see. Been in a scuffle with Ophelia's chimeras, have you?"

Miligan traced the origin of the injuries with just a glance. The demon ape bared its fangs at her and hissed menacingly. Oliver's hand shot to the athame at his waist. Unlike the creatures they'd encountered so far, this ape was clearly riled up.

"We mean you no harm, but it doesn't seem you're in the mood to listen... Oh well."

Miligan had sensed on this as well and was forced to give up on trying to pass by peacefully. Still ready to battle with the ape, she lifted the bangs that covered her left eye. The moment it spotted the basilisk eye, the ape's fur stood on end.

"So you won't back off even after seeing my eye. That means we have to fight—get ready, you three!" she barked and drew her athame. The intense staring contest continued, but the ape showed no sign of backing down. Seeing there was no avoiding combat, Oliver and Chela reached toward their waists.

"Wait a moment, Ms. Miligan."

A soft voice cooled their heads. The Azian girl stepped toward the demon ape, and Miligan's eyes bulged out of their sockets.

"...Nanao?"

"'Tis too early to draw. We have not paid our respects yet."

And immediately, Nanao got onto her knees. She removed her sword from her waist and placed it on the ground, facing the demon ape unarmed. Her back was straight as an arrow, and her three companions couldn't help but gape.

"We are in the middle of a journey to rescue a friend. Time is of the essence, and so we must rudely cut through your domain."

She spoke softly, remaining in position. After staring into her eyes for a few seconds, the ape suddenly leaned forward and brought its face closer to hers—close enough to bite her head off. It sniffed.

"Nanao...!"

"Wait, Chela!"

Chela, unable to watch, tried to draw her athame, but Oliver instinctively stopped her. Something was different. The situation appeared as dangerous as danger got, but the aggression the ape had displayed moments earlier had subsided.

"It is not my wish to open our path through violence. Will you grant us passage?"

Nanao expressed her desire directly, never breaking eye contact. Silence fell between the girl and the ape—until eventually, the ape slowly turned around. As her friends watched on, amazed, the demon ape returned to its nest, its back to them.

"...It withdrew...," Oliver said incredulously.

"Goodness... What trick did you use, Nanao?" Miligan excitedly asked, peering at the girl's face.

Nanao retied her sword to her waist, stood up, and replied. "According to Katie, most beast-like magical creatures determine an opponent's intentions from their mana and smell—things you and I emit unconsciously. The properties change based on our emotions. Thus, if one wishes to express that one is not a threat to such creatures, one must relax and face them with a still heart. The more excited they are, the calmer you must be—or so she claims."

She smiled as she said her friend's name. Chela crossed her arms and considered the surprising method.

"...Face them with a still heart, you say? I can see the logic, but... That's easier said than done against such a fierce creature..."

"But it makes sense," Oliver agreed. "The beast was injured and agitated, which is exactly why it'd want to avoid any unnecessary conflict. What you needed to convey was that you weren't a threat. I swear, you and Katie continue to surprise me."

He recalled the toolplant seeds he'd received from Guy. Even though they hadn't come along, Katie and Guy had still saved their butts. The entire group was working together to rescue Pete.

"...The Sword Roses, huh?" Oliver whispered.

Chela smiled next to him, and he grinned awkwardly. She was definitely thinking the same thing.

Miligan, after hearing Nanao's explanation, nodded vigorously. "Truly fascinating," she said. "In any case, we're lucky to avoid that fight. Now, let's hurry. Once we're through here, we still have to descend."

Miligan pointed ahead. The first-years followed her lead and resumed walking, but as soon as they were past the demon ape's nest, Oliver noticed a change above them.

"Ms. Miligan—the wyverns."

Their loyal followers had broken off and were now flying in a different direction. As the group looked up, they heard a loud sound behind them. They all jumped and turned around to see the demon ape from earlier bounding out of its nest. They tensed for battle, but the ape shot past them without a second glance.

"The boss ran away. Something's up over there."

Sensing something was amiss, Miligan took off. The three friends followed her when suddenly Oliver received a message via his secret mana frequency.

(Please be careful, my liege. A chimera is ahead!)

Oliver's face stiffened at Teresa's warning. Twenty more seconds of running and the path turned into a downward slope—and then he saw what she had warned him about.

Directly in their path, on a branch not far from the tree island, were two magical beasts locked in combat. On one side was the demon ape. On the other was a giant chimera about twice its size, a combination of half praying mantis, half beetle. Its two arms were giant scythes, and rows of segmented legs scuttled underneath its abdomen. On its thorax were multiple mounds of sharp needles. The demon ape howled and attacked, but the chimera held its ground.

"...A chimera is fighting with that ape...!" said Oliver.

"No wonder, when it looks like that and steps into the ape's territory."

Hiding in the twisted branches so as not to be spotted, the four of them watched the battle play out. The ape was fast despite its size, but for some reason, every time it got close to the chimera, a cloud of blood sprayed from its body. It hadn't been hit by the scythes, so how? Oliver's eyes and ears soon found the answer. Needles were sticking out of the ape's body. The chimera launched the needles on its thorax with alarming speed and an explosive noise.

Every time the ape approached, it got hit by another needle attack. And, unable to get close, the ape found its wounds growing more and more critical. On top of this, it was already injured, so the battle didn't last long. The ape sank to its knees after losing too much blood, and the chimera mercilessly brought down its scythe. With one blow, it decapitated the helpless irminsul ape.

"The western boss is dead, huh? I guess it was inevitable, considering it was injured, but this is trouble," Miligan muttered as she witnessed the conclusion of the fight. Oliver knew the meaning of what came next without her having to say it and swallowed hard.

"Killing the previous boss means this area is now that chimera's territory. And it's standing right in our way. We could technically withdraw and take a detour, but we'd have to be prepared for an attack on even worse footing... So what do we do?" Miligan turned to her juniors and asked. The three of them looked at one another for a second, then nodded in unison. If they were likely to fight anyway, it would be better to take a stand here than out on the branches where footing was poor. They were close enough to the "island" that they could lure the chimera there.

"I needn't have asked. Okay, have at it. I'll be the backup this time. You three defeat that chimera." Miligan nodded and took a step back, eyes glittering with expectation. She then added a piece of advice. "I'm sure you've already observed it, but this chimera is quite different from the one at the entrance to the second layer. This one's been designed to kill. Its strength and tactics differ totally—but most of all, if you lose, you die. Keep that in mind."

He was aware of this fact, but hearing it said out loud made the truth resonate deeply in Oliver's chest. His legs felt like they were about to give way, but he forced himself to stand and glared at their soon-to-be opponent.

"…It still hasn't noticed us. Should we continue observing it from a distance?" Chela asked.

"No. We've seen its body construction and witnessed it fight with another creature. As pressed for time as we are, we can't hope to gather much more information."

Oliver gave up on the idea and turned on his heel, heading for the island. Fortunately, it wasn't just spacious but was also covered in soil. *Lucky for us*, he thought as he looked down at the mulch underfoot.

"It's time to fight, you guys. We're gonna defeat that chimera."

He retrieved the toolplant seeds from his bag and spread them around the island.

"Brogoroccio!"

He cast a spell on the seeds, and one after the other, they began to sprout: In each spot, three trees grew to form short walls. Not only would these give them cover, but they would also help to slow down the large chimera. They weren't the sturdiest things, but it was better than nothing.

"…Everyone ready?" He turned and shouted, to which Nanao and Chela nodded sharply. Oliver raised his athame in the air.

"Fragor!"

A flash of light exploded above his head, signaling the beginning of the fight. The chimera, which was gorging itself on the ape's corpse, raised its insectoid head and immediately made a beeline for the island.

"Have at thee!"

Nanao stood in the center of the island, ready to receive it. The chimera struck first, swinging a scythe down at her. She dodged it by a hair, and Oliver shouted a warning:

"Here come those needles!"

As he'd anticipated, the chimera ejected its front-facing needles in response to Nanao's evasion. They were about eight inches long and seemed to be propelled by high-pressure gas. The needles flew so quickly that even the trio's magically reinforced robes couldn't protect them. A direct hit would mean at best a grievous wound and at worst lethal damage.

"Hah...!"

Nanao hid behind one of the plant walls; the needles struck it and remained buried inside, just as they'd hoped. Oliver let out a low, self-congratulatory "yes!" Nanao could probably deflect the needles with her sword, but as the fight was likely to drag on, there was far less risk of getting shot doing things this way.

"That's good! Don't rush it, Nanao!"

"Understood!" Nanao shouted back, then darted out from her cover. The chimera, its scythe poised to crush the wall, changed targets to Nanao and swung at her. She jumped to the side again, but this time there was no needle follow-up attack. It needed to recharge the gas inside its body before it could fire a second volley. Everything was just as they'd observed in its fight with the demon ape.

"Impetus!"

"Fragor!"

Oliver and Chela simultaneously cast offensive spells. Based on the chimera's construction, they deduced that its weak points would be focused on its upper half. Unfortunately, their spells bounced off it without any damage.

"Quite a tough body it's got…!"

"No surprise there! Tear off the exoskeleton and aim for its ganglion!"

Just as predicted, single-incantation spells had no effect on its outer shell. They quickly started casting their next spells, and the chimera turned its menacing glare toward them. But its attention was drawn to the ground, and the Azian girl made sure to take advantage of this opening.

"Your leg is mine!"

Nanao instantly dashed toward its feet and swung at the segmented insect leg before her. She severed the chimera's limb in half, and it fell to the ground.

"I knew you could do it, Nanao!"

"Mm!"

But one severed leg wasn't enough to destabilize the chimera. Unperturbed, it rained needles down from its giant body. Nanao once again dived behind a wall, narrowly escaping. Oliver's expression grew tense. She dodged this time, but the farther she stepped in, the higher the risk of being shot. But worst of all, a new leg was already sprouting from the severed segment.

"Of course it regenerates…," Oliver muttered. "And because it was designed for combat, it regenerates quickly, too."

"If it can't be destabilized, then the risk isn't worth the reward. Avoid aiming for the legs, Nanao," Chela called.

"Understood. So this is the trial-and-error method, eh?"

Higher risks didn't necessarily come with higher rewards. Having personally experienced this and learned from her mistake, the Azian girl raised her sword again. The chimera's attention was still on her, as if looking for revenge for its severed leg. Oliver and Chela took this as their opening.

"Flamma!"

"Frigus!"

Spells of fire and ice—reading their opponent's movements, they aimed the opposite-element spells at the same spot, one after the other. The chimera's exoskeleton burned, then instantly froze. Immediately, they followed up with another spell simultaneously.

"'Fragor!'"

This time, they cast an explosion spell on the previously damaged area, and amid the blasts, they heard a dry, cracking sound. They swallowed and looked up—a section of the exoskeleton was missing, like a broken piece of pottery, revealing a yellow internal organ.

"We broke it! Weakening the exoskeleton with the temperature worked!" cried Chela.

"Blast it with magic before it can recover! Tonitrus!"

The pair quickly struck again. But after two hits, the chimera had learned, and it sharply swung its body to avoid the blow. Their spells hit a solid piece of exoskeleton and fizzled. At the same time, a scythe cleaved toward them, definitely capable of cutting them in half. They wisely jumped backward to dodge.

"It's protecting the damaged area...!"

"But it can't recover the exoskeleton as quickly! If we crack more of in its armor, we can do this!" Chela replied, putting a positive spin on the situation. She resumed casting, and Oliver cast in tandem without missing a beat.

Miligan watched the battle unfold from a nearby branch.

"...Yes. Yes. Good—very good," she muttered delightedly as the three underclassmen darted about. Their first battle with a chimera was far exceeding her expectations.

"Thanks to Nanao drawing its attacks, Oliver and Chela can experiment much more. And their decision to remove the chimera's exoskeleton first after observing its movements was totally correct. Not to mention how quickly they stopped aiming for the legs after discovering the risk wasn't worth it."

Her smile deepened. Compared to when they'd first fought,

the Azian girl's movements were sharper, and the boy had much improved. Chela didn't disappoint, either. They were still quite inexperienced, but they had improved remarkably.

"I'm very impressed that after only one lesson, you've come this far. Your adaptability is remarkable. But I wonder if you realize—the moment you see victory in a battle with an unknown opponent is also the most dangerous."

The fighting continued for over ten minutes. As the last of Oliver's toolplant walls fell, the battle entered its final phase.

"It just won't die! We've blasted its guts more than ten times, and it's still kicking...!"

"No, it's definitely working!" Oliver shouted back to Chela. "The chimera's shooting a lot fewer needles. Time for the final blow!"

Seeing that their opponent was out of ammo, Oliver made the decision to finish it off. The needles were created within the chimera's body, so it couldn't possibly have an infinite stock. Not only had it already used tons of them in their battle, but it had probably wasted more during its fight with the demon ape.

There were at least ten or so holes in the chimera's exoskeleton, and its movements were slowing thanks to the internal damage dealt by Oliver's and Chela's spells. It was the perfect opportunity to finish it, Oliver was sure, as he barked orders to the girls.

"I'll distract it from the front! You two circle around to the sides!"

"Got it!"

"Understood!"

Oliver took Nanao's place in front of the chimera. The injured beast bellowed, and the girls attacked together from the sides.

"Fragor!"

"Haaaaah!"

Chela's explosion spell was deafening; Nanao decided to attack the chimera's legs again. Without its needles, the chimera was forced to swipe at its enemies with its scythes. They just barely dodged—just as Oliver dashed right in its face.

"Brogoroccio."

He scattered the seeds from his left hand and chanted a spell. At first, nothing happened. The chimera quickly noticed him and swung its head down straight at him. All out of needles and its arms preoccupied, its only choice was to attack the prey under its nose with its mandibles. Oliver activated Grave Step underneath his feet, shooting backward and dodging the attack by a hair.

"Hissss?!"

Toolplants shot up from both sides simultaneously, locking the chimera's head in place. Oliver's delayed cast meant the spell took a while to activate. Unable to move, the chimera's defenseless upper body was exposed to Oliver. From the very beginning, he'd suspected that based on the chimera's template body, the location of its supraesophageal ganglion—the core of its life functions—had to be...

"Here!"

He slipped into the gap between the chimera's head and the ground, glaring at his enemy's weak spot right before his eyes. It was almost over. He quickly raised his athame.

"—!"

The next moment, just as he was about to plunge in his blade, a bundle of needles appeared as if to mock his attempt.

The all-too-familiar sound of high-pressure gas. That was all Miligan needed to understand what had just happened.

"Aw, and so close, too. He took it head-on after all."

With a sigh, she drew her athame and jumped off the branch from which she'd been observing. The battle had been so fantastic up to that point that she couldn't help but be terribly disappointed in her juniors' failure to finish the job.

"But I don't blame him. It's a dirty trick; Ophelia always designs her

chimeras with the assumption that their weak points will be discovered... Try not to die immediately, Oliver. I'll be right there to save you—"

But Miligan stopped ten yards short of joining the fray. What she saw made not only her human eye but even her basilisk eye as well open wide in surprise.

"...Ha-ha. You've gotta be kidding me."

"I predicted that, too."

Oliver taunted his foe as he wielded a chunk of its exoskeleton in his left hand as a shield, blocking the chimera's final surprise attack. He'd predicted this from the middle of the battle, when he'd carved off a chunk of the leg Nanao had severed and snuck it under his robe. Pieces removed from the chimera's body deteriorated quickly, but he could keep it fresh with spatial magic. There was no guarantee the small shield would block all the needles, but at the very least, he'd bet on it protecting his vital organs.

"HISSSSSSSSS!"

The chimera howled as if it knew the end was near. Its final trap disarmed, the creature had no means of fighting back anymore.

"*Frigus!*"

Oliver plunged his athame into the beast all the way up to the blade's guard and cast the spell, intending to put an end to things once and for all. Freezing energy rushed from the tip of the athame into the chimera's body, freezing in a matter of seconds the organs that controlled its life functions. The light flickered out of the chimera's eyes. Oliver jumped back just as its giant body collapsed limply.

"...Is it...dead?" Chela asked, witnessing victory but still unwilling to put down her sword. Oliver looked at the corpse for a few seconds, then cast another spell in the same spot for good measure.

"Yeah, it's dead," he replied with a confident nod. "I froze and destroyed its ganglion. It's totally dead."

The tension in his body released, and all at once, Oliver felt incredibly heavy. Nanao rushed at him excitedly, completely unaffected.

"Excellent work, Oliver!"

"Same to you, Nanao."

They bumped their right arms together. Finally, reality washed over Oliver.

"And you too, Chel— Ahh?!"

"Hrm?!"

Oliver and Nanao turned to include their friend, but they were in for a big surprise: She flung herself at them, squeezing their bodies together in an embrace.

"...We won...! We defeated it! The three of us defeated that terrible chimera!"

Her voice was shaking with elation. They basked in the joy of victory as Miligan walked over, clapping.

"Congratulations on your first victory. For your first time, I'm quite impressed. I could barely pick my jaw up off the ground."

"Ms. Miligan..."

"Honestly, I would've given you a passing grade just for ripping off the chimera's exoskeleton and exhausting it. If Nanao had tried to unleash her special technique or Chela had been forced to use her elf form, I would've stepped in... But this? Looking back on it, I know there was never a chance for me to help. I just had to sit there, spinning my wheels."

She sounded disappointed, but her lips were unmistakably curved into a smile. She was simply glad to see her juniors outdoing her expectations.

"Now, shall we keep moving? It seems your adventure doesn't end here."

Miligan took the lead again, praising the trio's growth. And with newfound confidence in their hearts, the three first-years followed.

CHAPTER 3

Salvadori, the Succubus Progeny

"…Hey, look."

"Yeah, that's her. I've heard the rumors…"

The gazes of the other students on her were always a mix of emotions—fear and jealousy, curiosity and disgust—ever since Ophelia had joined Kimberly.

"It's like her smell is sucking me in…"

"Whoa, don't get too close! She'll kidnap you."

"Is it true that she'll make babies with anyone?"

"Only 'cause it's better than having sex with a monster."

Back then, some were still foolish enough to talk about her within earshot. It was annoying, but she ignored it like background noise. Her disdain for her peers grew as well; she supposed that the lower one's bloodline and intellect, the more likely one was to gossip in little huddles.

"U-um, Ms. Salvadori…"

"What?"

Sometimes people called out to her, and she responded in the manner her disdain commanded. As a result, most ran away after she shot them an icy glare. For half of her first year at Kimberly, Ophelia didn't talk to anyone except Carlos.

"Still no friends, Lia?"

"…Shut up."

Carlos, who'd entered the academy a year earlier, spent as much time with her as they could. On this day in particular, the two of them took lunch in an empty classroom. Ophelia hated the cafeteria and its droves of students most of all, and so she chose to eat in placcs away from the eyes of others.

"I can understand that the Salvadori name might keep people away, but you're still distancing yourself too much. Why don't you try being a bit a more friendly? That ought to strike someone's fancy."

"I don't need friends. I can attract as many men as I want. That's good enough."

She munched on a cheese muffin. The faint hope Carlos had for her before she started school had completely dissipated in the past six months, and she'd withdrawn from nearly all contact with others.

Carlos shook their head, troubled. "*You* say it's fine, but I don't. I want to see you laughing in the middle of a group of friends. That's been my dream ever since the day we met."

"Keep your creepy dreams to yourself… Anyway, I don't care. I'm not making any friends."

She tossed her half-eaten muffin into the basket and turned away from them, pouting. Carlos studied her profile and sank into thought.

"…All right. But what about *my* friends? I can at least introduce you, right?"

"Do what you want. I'll just ignore them," she stated coldly, still not looking Carlos's way.

But Carlos smiled. They had her word now. They promptly turned and left the classroom, then came back with another student in tow before Ophelia had a chance to process anything.

"Here we go. Al, this is Ophelia. Introduce yourself."

"Right."

At Carlos's urging, the boy stepped in front of Ophelia. He was tall, with broad, muscular shoulders; his black hair was so stiff that it seemed to resist any curling; and his dark eyes stared uncomfortably straight into hers. Intimidated by his silent pressure, Ophelia found herself shifting backward in her seat.

"I am Alvin Godfrey, a second-year. It is nice to meet you, Ophelia.

I hope you'll forgive my forwardness—I was told you dislike being called by your last name."

Godfrey introduced himself quite formally, then gave a surprisingly soft smile. He immediately stuck out his right hand for a handshake; Ophelia stared at him like a rare creature.

"……"

"Carlos has told me a lot about you. I realize I'm only a year older, but that still makes you my junior, so please don't hesitate to reach out if you're having any trouble adjusting to— Hmm?"

His fluid speech came to a halt. A few seconds of silence passed; then the boy calmly did an about-face and drew his wand.

"Dolor!"

His back to Ophelia, he cast a pain curse on his crotch. His tall frame collapsed dramatically to its knees.

"…Guh… Haaa…!"

"…Huh? …What?! W-wait, what're you doing?!"

Ophelia jumped from her chair in a slight panic, not understanding what had just happened. Godfrey was on the ground, gritting his teeth and supporting himself with shaky arms. Sweat poured down his brow as he struggled to get up.

"…I'm terribly sorry. A despicable sensation arose within me, but I managed to quell it with the pain of a kick in the groin, so please forgive me."

She gaped at him. Was he an idiot? No one had asked him to go to such extremes.

Godfrey wobbled to his feet and took deep breaths to recover from his self-inflicted punishment.

As Ophelia stared at him in awe, Carlos whispered in her ear, "… See? Unique, isn't he?"

"……"

That much was true, she was willing to admit. Everything else aside, there was no doubting that point. It was unlikely you'd find a single other person in the magical world stupid enough to punish themselves with a pain curse unbidden. Godfrey let out a big breath, then turned back to Ophelia, a calm expression on his face. He extended his hand again as if nothing had happened.

"Your Perfume was more intense than I anticipated... But a bit of mental fortitude renders it powerless. It's nice to meet you, Ophelia."

He snorted and puffed out his chest, as if to say, *Bring it on.*

Ophelia was so caught off guard she burst into laughter for the first time in her life.

Her first impression of him was that he was an unprecedented idiot. But it turned out she was wrong—she would come to find that Alvin Godfrey was an *astronomical* idiot.

"Good morning, Ophelia. Would you care for breakf— **Dolor!**"

"Good evening, Ophelia. Have you figured out how to use the libr— **Dolor!**"

"Ophelia, look! A fairy nest, here of all— **Dolor!**"

Ever since becoming acquainted, Godfrey would repeat this routine without fail whenever they ran into each other on campus. It didn't bother him that others might be watching. And of course, he always finished the routine by falling to his knees. Ophelia realized that this was his way of suppressing the lust her Perfume inspired, but his methods and persistence were clearly abnormal. He knew seeing her would cause him to writhe in pain, yet he always did exactly that once every two days. He was so stubborn, in fact, that she started to suspect it was a fetish of his.

Each instance would inspire an uproar in the nearby students, focusing unneeded attention on her, so of course Ophelia found his antics a huge nuisance. Yet, she never stopped him. Perhaps she was curious to see how far this idiot would go—to see what heights his foolishness would reach.

"Good day, Ophelia. Eating lunch?"

"Uh, yes..."

About two months had passed since they were first introduced. Ophelia was sitting on a bench in a corner of the school courtyard. This was their thirtieth meeting, and she once again prepared herself for what she was sure was to come.

"…Heh-heh-heh-heh-heh…"

"…?"

But it didn't come. Godfrey sat next to her and began chuckling creepily. She eyed him suspiciously as he balled his hands into fists.

"…I've won. I've finally conquered my instincts through pain!" he crowed with accomplishment. Ophelia stared at him wide-eyed. She couldn't believe it—the idiot had finally done it.

What specifically he'd done was imprint a conditioned reflex. Every time they met and sexual excitement arose within him, he'd extinguish the lust with a pain curse. Repeating this process over a long period of time caused his body to remember that experiencing sexual feelings for her would result in extreme pain.

"Now we can get to know each other better, and I'll be able to give you advice. Talk to me about anything, Ophelia. The man who would pass out from pain while gripping his crotch upon seeing you is long gone. Before you now is a new Alvin Godfrey!"

"U-um…"

He grabbed her hand and vigorously shook it; Ophelia's brain seemed to stop working. Realizing what he was doing, Godfrey quickly let go.

"Sorry. I allowed my elation to get the better of me. Let's start again: May I eat lunch with you? Feel free to say no if you'd rather be alone."

And with his usual candor, he asked to join her. He was the epitome of seriousness. Ophelia swallowed—eventually, she managed to gasp out a question.

"…Why…?"

"Hmm?"

"…Why did you try so hard? There must have been a hundred easier ways."

She asked quite frankly. What she'd considered most idiotic of all was that his efforts held no meaning. There were much simpler, more logical ways to achieve the same results—potions or spells that would increase his resistance, for instance. In fact, even if he became aroused, he could simply keep a cool face, and no one would be able to tell the difference. And if lusting for her was the problem, then he could just stay away from her to begin with. No matter what angle you considered it from, he'd chosen the most painful, pointless path of his own volition. That was all she could think.

Godfrey crossed his arms and *hmm*'d to himself. "...Indeed, I see what you're saying. I don't think I chose the best method, either. I mean, every time I thought of going to see you these past two months, my body would shiver. If I saw a friend doing the same thing, I'd certainly stop them."

She was surprised to hear that he was self-aware. Godfrey's expression turned solemn.

"But the pain I experienced these past two months—it's nothing compared to what you've endured your entire life."

"...!"

It was like a shot to the heart. So many people had avoided her because they disliked the effects of her Perfume. Meanwhile, Godfrey was the first person other than Carlos to consider the pain she'd experienced, having been born this way.

"So I don't mind," he said. "The pain doesn't bother me if it allows me to sit proudly next to you."

He flashed a friendly grin. After a long silence, Ophelia spoke again.

"...Then what do you want, sitting next to such a difficult girl?"

It was a mean-spirited question. Godfrey's expression turned to surprise.

"Difficult? You? ...Ha-ha-ha! That's hilarious!"

He burst into laughter and slapped his knee. Ophelia eyed him suspiciously, so he stifled his laughter and faced her again.

"Listen, Ophelia: a truly difficult person would never even think such a thing. They would simply laugh and go for the kill. I had three such experiences in the latter half of last year. Two of those times, I nearly died! My blood boils just remembering it."

Suddenly, unbridled anger appeared on his face. She wanted to ask what happened, but Godfrey calmed himself and returned his gaze to her.

"So that's why you were distant, then? Well, I suppose you did see me at my worst multiple times. But it was all of my own volition. You have no reason to feel guilty. So for the third time: Shall we have lunch?"

She hesitated for a second, then nodded. Godfrey smiled; he picked up the basket he'd placed on the bench and put it on his lap.

"Then let's chat. How are your classes? The magical biology instructor is a beast, isn't she?"

He began making idle chatter.

The boy sitting next to her was supposed to be an idiot who never learned. Yet, for some reason, lunch period that day seemed unbearably short for Ophelia.

✳

Pete contemplated ways of breaking out of the dark cell, but it was soon apparent that this task would be impossible on his own. He was completely unarmed, with neither a wand nor any sort of tool, so there was no logical way of escaping this older student's prison. With that in mind, he decided on his next course of action.

"...Hey. Hey, wake up...!"

He set about trying to shake his fellow prisoners awake. Having an ally might create an opportunity—it was a slim chance, but he had to bet on it.

Unfortunately, his efforts were in vain. They refused to wake up, even if he pinched their butts or slapped their faces. After ten tries, he was done. He nearly despaired but convinced himself the eleventh time might be the charm and put all his might into pinching their cheek—and finally, something changed.

"...Mm...?"

"Oh... You're awake?! Yes! Don't go back to sleep! Don't go back to sleep!" Pete called with desperate hope at the first student to show any sort of reaction. It seemed to work, as their eyes began focusing before eventually settling on Pete's face.

"You're...one of the nobodies...in Oliver's group. Where...?"

Pete gasped upon hearing those words. He hadn't realized because of the dark and his desperation, but this was Joseph Albright, the boy Oliver had fought in the first-years' battle royale. The memory of the swarm of bees was still fresh in his mind. Pete was suddenly not so relieved. Albright lifted himself up and looked about, his expression growing grim.

"...Salvadori's workshop, huh? Damn, of all the rotten luck!" Realizing the situation, he searched his whole body. "She took our athames and wands, of course. Anything else— Ugh!"

"A-are you okay?!"

Albright suddenly paused and held his head.

Pete jumped closer, but Albright stopped him with a hand.

"Don't squawk. I'm perfectly fine," Albright said. "Deep breaths cause me to inhale air dripping with her Perfume. Even my extraordinary resistance to poison and charms isn't enough...," he explained, steadying his breathing.

He eyed Pete suspiciously. "...Hey, shrimp. How are you able to move?"

"Huh...?"

"You don't realize it, do you? ...Look at the other sleeping fools. That's the typical reaction down here. No man can resist her Perfume. Even I wouldn't have awoken if not for you disturbing me. Yet, here you are, moving about unhindered in this miasma. I find that hard to reconcile."

Pete was unsure how to respond. He could smell the peculiar scent in the air, but it didn't make him sleepy. If the other students were exhibiting the Perfume's natural effects, then why was he the only one unaffected?

Suddenly, he gasped.

"...Oh..."

Unconsciously, he searched his body. Finding his assumption to be true, he stiffened. Albright, who watched this whole act unfold, narrowed his eyes in understanding.

"Ah, I see. You're not a man, are you?"

A great panic came over Pete. But after a moment, he realized this was no time to be keeping secrets. He hesitated, then revealed what was going on with his body.

Albright snorted. "Hmph, a reversi. Not something you'd expect from a nobody. But now I understand—Salvadori's chimera mistook you for a male and captured you. Then, after you were brought here and put to sleep, you changed into a female. Since the charm effect is weaker on the same sex, you broke free and awakened. That about sums it up."

"I-if you get what's happening, then help me escape! There has to be a way— Mgh?!"

Pete started to shout in excitement, but Albright covered his mouth with a hand.

"Shut up. You don't understand the mess you're in. If you're found, you'll be killed."

"...!"

"Your presence is an unexpected problem for Salvadori. Our value to her is as males. That's why she brought us here." Albright calmly spelled it out, still covering Pete's mouth.

Pete listened in silence, feeling like someone had just dumped ice water on his head.

"Given her unsophisticated methods, Salvadori's likely lost her sanity. We can't expect the rarity of a reversi to incite her curiosity, nor her to show any compassion for her juniors. The proof is over there."

Albright finally removed his hand from Pete's mouth and shot a look outside the flesh cage. Pete turned his head in the same direction and saw what had caused him to shiver earlier—a bunch of students were nailed to the wall, their clothes shredded and flesh "pipes" connected to various points on their bodies. Among them was one of the students his friends had battled recently.

"...Mr. Willock..."

"Unlike you, the vitality of a half-werewolf makes him a perfect target. We're all here to end up like him, then disposed of when we're no longer of any use."

When Albright stated the naked truth, Pete swallowed and went silent.

"You understand, then? Good. If we take the initiative, we can turn the tables. No one could've predicted you would be able to move around freely in this miasma. You're our trump card."

Now that they were both on the same page, Albright began discussing how they could escape. Pete looked at him hopefully; then Albright calmly stabbed his fingers into his side and winced.

"Wh-what the—?!" Pete exclaimed.

"Shut up and watch!"

Albright fished around inside his own guts, eventually producing several small spheres. Something seemed to be sealed inside the glass balls—four different colors. The bloody balls sat in Albright's palm.

"For when my wand's been taken from me. Two of these are explosive—infuse them with mana and they'll cause a small but destructive explosion. We'll use these to escape this cell. The other two are a smoke screen, which reduces visibility and will provide us an opportunity to get away, as well as a rescue signal—it emits a loud sound as well as mana to try and call an ally for help."

Pete listened in awe. Albright stuck his hand out in front of the bespectacled boy's nose.

"I'm giving them all to you. They're worthless to me to have them in this state."

"...Oh..."

Pete reflexively held out his hands and accepted the eight glass spheres. He could feel the lingering warmth from Albright's guts on them. Pete stood, feeling like he'd just been entrusted with a massive responsibility.

"Wait for your chance," Albright continued sternly. "Until Salvadori leaves the workshop, hopefully when she gets as far away as possible. I'm certain that a search party of upperclassmen has been dispatched to this layer of the labyrinth. If we can just alert them to our position, the tables should turn."

That was their single greatest hope. Now that Pete knew the plan, Albright suddenly remembered something. "I suppose I should ask your name, shrimp, seeing as I'm entrusting my life to you. What is it?"

"...Pete Reston," the bespectacled boy answered stiffly. Albright snorted.

"Pete, then. If we make it out of this alive, I'll remember that."

The giant chimera shook the ground with its weight as it proceeded through the forest, knocking down trees as it went. A slight distance away, in the shadow of a tree, two students watched with bated breath.

"...It's finally gone. Woo, that was scary!"

One was taller than the other and appeared to be an older female student. The girl next to her got up off the ground and set out with purpose, practically stomping through the forest. The tall girl quickly chased after her.

"Hey! Be a little more careful! We'll be in major trouble if we're spotted."

"There's no time! I have to save Fay!"

The panicked girl was another of the participants in the battle royale, one who gave Chela a run for her money: Stacy Cornwallis. Just as Oliver and the others had lost Pete to the chimera, she had lost her half-werewolf partner, Fay Willock. After catching up to her, the tall girl sighed dramatically.

"I know already, okay? …Ugh, it was a mistake bringing you along. I should've known something was up when someone as disrespectful as you actually came to me begging for help."

The complaints were coming from a girl named Lynette Cornwallis, Stacy's sister and three years her elder. Lynette pursed her lips, miffed by her younger sister's insistence on charging into danger.

"…You sure are attached to your little pet. Is he seriously that precious to you? He's just a stray puppy you happened to find one day. You could easily repla—"

Stacy snapped around and glared daggers at her sister. Lynette raised her hands in surrender.

"…Guess not. Yeah, yeah. I'm sorry."

Stacy silently turned back and proceeded forward once more. It was the perfect opportunity to stop talking, but Lynette didn't seem to learn.

"What I don't get is that no matter how much you care for him, you're never gonna bear his children. You could get any man you wanted, being a Cornwallis. Father may dislike you, but you're still our family's beacon of hope."

"……"

"Or are you thinking of abandoning the family altogether? Forsake us to become a McFarlane? That's why you're trying to cuddle up to Uncle Theodore, isn't it? …Well, I wish you luck. No matter how precocious you might be, you'll never bring down Ms. Michela and replace her—"

She was clearly taunting Stacy, trying to provoke her, but her sister refused to respond. Lynette clicked her tongue.

"Could you quit ignoring me for, like, one second? …*Sigh*. What are you, mute? I always tried to talk to you at home, but you basically never responded."

She hazily recalled a time long ago, when Michela McFarlane came to visit: her little sister gifting a flower crown she'd made to this girl from the main family, who was considered a prodigy.

Michela had seemed genuinely delighted; Stacy had been blushing furiously. They were a greater picture of sisterly love than Lynette could ever paint with Stacy.

"…You could've made me one, too."

"…?"

Stacy picked up on her older sister's mutterings and turned around questioningly. Lynette shrugged, averting her eyes in an attempt to avoid Stacy's gaze.

"It's nothing. Let's get moving. You're in a hurry, right?"

Meanwhile, Oliver's group had reached the second layer's end.

"All right, time to wrap up this layer," Miligan said, leading the way. They'd already made it through the forest, and the shrubbery was growing smaller by the minute. Chela, upon noticing that there was bare dirt beneath her feet, raised her eyebrows in suspicion.

"…The vegetation has practically disappeared. I don't sense any living things, either."

"Yeah, but there's still soil. Odd… Ms. Miligan, what's going on?" Oliver asked, also sensing that something was off.

Miligan stopped. "I could explain, but you know what they say: Seeing is believing."

The next moment, the ground beneath their feet began to shake slightly. Puzzled, Oliver looked down to see arms of white bone breaking through the soil.

"Wha—?!"

He jumped back in shock, but that was only the beginning. Pale bones were bursting out of the ground as far as the eye could see. From the shifting earth appeared skeleton warriors clad in battered armor and wielding swords and spears. There were easily thousands of them. Chela stared in awe at the scores of undead suddenly appearing without warning.

"Spartoi...?! And so many of them!" she exclaimed.

"Quite the sight, isn't it? Relax. They're on our side."

Miligan was surprisingly calm. Oliver and the girls didn't immediately grasp what she was saying; the witch cast a spell at the ground, creating a medium-size platform, then hopped on top and surveyed the far side of the undead army.

"Our opponents are getting into position as well. Study each side's battle formations carefully, now."

Confused, they decided to copy Miligan and hopped up on the magically created platform for a better view. Far in the distance, beyond the army of skeletons, they could see another group of bony warriors rising from the earth. Each side's armor bore different designs, and they faced each other in orderly formation.

"They're forming battle lines with weapons in hand—this is a battle."

"Correct answer, Nanao. This is the final trial for the second layer—the Battle of Hell's Armies," Miligan revealed excitedly, then turned slowly back to the other three. "Let me sum up the rules for you: There are two armies of spartoi before you, and you will be fighting alongside one of those armies. Your goal is to lead your forces to victory. More specifically, the moment you destroy the enemy general is the moment you win. If your general falls, you lose."

Oliver swallowed. They were expected to jump into battle among this ocean of skeletons? Miligan ignored his apprehension and continued explaining: "It's hidden behind the enemy army, but if you win, the door to the third layer will open. But be careful: Riding broomsticks is against the rules. Doing so is an instant loss, so remember that. If you lose, the next battle won't start for another three hours. Also, if you leave your army to its own devices, it's guaranteed to lose. The point of this game is to overturn that result with your own strength. Think hard and fight hard!"

And with that, she swept past her stunned juniors. They watched her go, and when she'd gone twenty yards she turned and settled back to observe.

"Sorry, but I can't help. I've already cleared this trial this year. Do it once, and you're free to pass through for a whole year. But in exchange, you can't participate in the game anymore."

A hint of worry rose to Oliver's face. In other words, the three of them had to surpass this trial on their own merits.

"If things look dire, I'll step in and save you. At that point, you should ignore the rules and run. Before you're killed by enemy troops, of course," she added nonchalantly, just as the deep sound of a horn bellowed across the battlefield.

"That's the horn. You have five minutes to strategize."

And with that last piece of advice, she shut her mouth for good. The three first-years immediately jumped into a huddle, not wanting to waste a second.

"If this game is a mock battle, then it's essentially just like chess," said Chela. "We should start by checking each side's pieces!"

"Agreed," Oliver replied. "Don't forget to note each side's formations and the surrounding terrain!"

They nodded and split up. After scoping out the battlefield, the trio regrouped.

"'Tis a flat field. No geographical formations of note. Both sides seem about equal in strength, but I counted more mounted soldiers on their flanks."

"In exchange, we have some other type of unit in our front line…"

"Judging from their size and skeletal structure, I'd say they're swordrhinos, a type of magical beast," said Oliver. "We can use them to mow down the enemy's vanguard and, once their formation is broken, follow up with our infantry… That's my analysis as a layman, at least."

Oliver was hardly confident in himself, but he offered his opinion. A mage duel was nothing compared to a battle of this scale, so he was completely out of his element. He didn't even know if his analysis was correct.

Chela seemed to be equally unsure. "We do appear to be lacking in horses; I have no knowledge of nonmagical battles, so I can't say for sure if that's a definite disadvantage. Ms. Miligan said we're guaranteed to lose if we do nothing. Nanao, do you have any idea why that would be?"

"Mm…"

The only one they could rely on was Nanao, who had experience in similar battles. Her friends gulped and watched as she crossed her arms and thought for a full ten seconds.

"…Mm, I haven't the slightest idea! I have never been a general, after all!" she finally piped up, her expression bright. Oliver's shoulders drooped in disappointment, but Chela quickly recovered.

"There's no need for us to pretend to be generals," she explained. "Our goal is simple: slay the enemy general. That's all we have to think about."

This gave Oliver hope. She was right—he couldn't let himself get distracted by the decorum. They were still mages, after all.

"…From what I saw, the soldiers surrounding the general are tough," said Oliver. "Most likely they're imperial guards. Their equipment is different from the other soldiers', and they've got an insane amount of mana. If we attack recklessly, we'll certainly be beaten back."

"Our only chance is to attack once both sides clash and the battle becomes a brawl. If we can get within spellcasting range, I'll finish this in one shot," Chela announced with confidence. The other two nodded, and the horn blew again.

"We're out of time… Let's go with Chela's plan. Be careful not to get caught up in the frontline clash. Maintain your distance and wait for the perfect chance to strike down the enemy general. Got it, Nanao?"

The Azian girl nodded. At the same time, the skeletal swordrhinos on their vanguard began charging forward.

"It's started…!"

The skeletal beasts thundered forward and kicked up dust in their wake. Their charge was clearly an attempt to get in the first strike, just as Oliver had predicted. But the next moment, his expectations were shattered.

As they watched, the enemy lines that should have been crushed under the swordrhinos' attack instead moved quickly, opening up a path for them. The swordrhinos charged in, as if the enemy lines were a giant throat—and ended up flying out the opposite side of the enemy army, without inflicting any damage.

"...My word! They passed right through!"

"Indeed, they were prepared for the charge. Such tactics are indicative of a talented general."

Chela was shocked, but Nanao appeared oddly impressed. Oliver, however, was feeling quite similarly to Chela. At the same time, there was a nagging feeling in the back of his mind that something was off.

"...?"

As he grappled with the uncertainty, this time the mounted units from both sides clashed. Even Oliver knew that their side was at a disadvantage, numbers-wise, but reality was even more terrible. Their units were pushed back in the initial clash, and this seemed to demoralize them as they turned tail and ran.

"Our mounted units have been pushed back as well...! Can we be any worse off?!"

"We clearly can't keep watching from the sidelines!" Chela shouted. "I'll support our troops—**Fragor!**"

With the swordrhinos' charge nullified and their cavalry defeated, all they could rely on now was their main force of footmen. Both sides clashed with spears and shields in hand; meanwhile, spells arced overhead as Chela and Oliver offered support. The explosion spells landed in the middle of the enemy's lines and detonated, blowing up a bunch of skeletal soldiers. Unfortunately, the resulting hole was immediately filled by the rear soldiers, and there was no effect on the army's momentum.

"…No use! A battle of this size can't be affected by tiny spell strikes!" said Oliver.

"Then shall I join at the front—?"

"Stop, Nanao! If the situation gets that bad, then we should just run!" Chela yelled back.

The Azian girl attempted to join the battle as if it was second nature, but her friends grabbed her by the shoulders and stopped her. But as they fumbled for their next move, the state of the battle changed before their eyes. Their front line completely mowed down, the rear line moved up to take their place—halting the enemy's advance.

"Wait," said Oliver. "Something's wrong."

"The front line crumbled, yet the back line isn't giving ground," Nanao explained. "Our best soldiers must have been placed there beforehand."

And just as she described, the new lines of soldiers were fighting hard. Their round shields locked tightly together, they pushed back at the enemy, not letting them take a single step forward.

"They're pushing them back!" Chela shouted excitedly. "This isn't over yet!"

"……"

Oliver, however, was still nursing that lingering feeling from earlier. It was growing stronger, from a nameless niggling into a single, coherent answer.

"…The Battle of Diama," he muttered. The girls turned to him.

"…What did you just say, Oliver?"

"The Battle of Diama—it was an ancient battle between two great nations, in year 300 of the Old Calendar, and became the deciding battle in the long war between Rumoa and Kurtoga. I remember Pete telling me about this."

Oliver searched his memories as he spoke. He could only recall the battle in bits and pieces; it came up randomly in conversation, so it was hard to remember what exactly Pete had said about it.

"I know those two names," Chela replied. "They both fell before the Union was formed."

"Yeah. Not many mages are well versed in military history, but among nonmagicals, it's apparently pretty popular."

Oliver nodded as he recalled this particular detail. In ancient times, when there were far fewer mages, wars between nations were often decided depending on one's use of nonmagical soldiers. The Battle of Diama in particular was a clash between two famous generals deeply connected by fate.

"The flow of that battle matches up perfectly with what we just saw. If it's not a coincidence—then this is a reproduction."

Oliver closed his eyes and focused on searching his memories. Pete's uncharacteristically talkative voice resurfaced vividly in his ears.

"Rumoa's general, after experiencing heavy losses in earlier battles due to flanking maneuvers from Kurtoga's cavalry, attempted to lure them into a trap. Knowing this, the Kurtoga general instead placed his swordrhinos at the front—but thanks to excellent maneuvering on Rumoa's part, the swordrhinos' charge was nullified by simply creating a space for them to run through. See, it's almost impossible for swordrhinos to change direction once they've accelerated to ramming speed. And with their lack of training, most of the swordrhinos couldn't even return to the fight."

Oliver relayed everything he could remember to Nanao and Chela, who listened quietly.

"However, Kurtoga's general wasn't content to take this lying down. In order to avoid a head-on clash while his cavalry were outnumbered, he chose to withdraw his cavalry first. This was to lure the enemy's greatest threat—its cavalry—to the sides."

"Ah, so it *was* a strategy." Nanao nodded, convinced. Their disappointingly quick retreat was a ruse to draw the enemy's cavalry away from its main force.

Oliver continued, sharing in her opinion: "As a result, the battle came down to a clash between the remaining footmen. Kurtoga was on the back foot, but thanks to the efforts of their skillful soldiers, they managed to change the tide of battle. Thus, the battle formation drew out into one long line—which is where we are now."

He paused to catch his breath. Chela, understanding what this signified, picked up where he left off. "So our forces are Kurtoga, and the enemy is Rumoa. But—what happens next?"

This was the most important part. Oliver searched his memory some more.

"...Our forces drove Rumoa to within an inch of defeat," he continued. "However, while this was happening, Kurtoga's cavalry were defeated. Rumoa's cavalry returned to the battle, piercing their ranks from behind. Within a matter of seconds, their formation was destroyed—and the battle decided."

The history lesson stopped there. With all the information now available to them, he attempted to connect it to their current situation.

"In other words—if we don't stop the enemy cavalry from returning, history will repeat itself, and we'll lose."

The conclusion he reached was quite simple. The three of them turned around, their eyes fixated on the cavalry positioned away from the main battlefield. Although outnumbered, their forces were faithfully fulfilling their orders to draw out the enemy's cavalry. It wouldn't be long before they were decimated, however.

"How do we overturn this?"

"Nothing comes to mind immediately. Nanao, any ideas?!"

"Hmm. With only three of us, the only way to stop the enemy's charge would be...with magic, I daresay," Nanao answered honestly, drawing from her experience on the battlefield. The situation was bleak enough to make even the greatest strategist throw in the towel, yet Oliver clenched his fist. He wouldn't accept this.

"Yeah. But we're mages—there must be a way," he said firmly. The girls quickly shared in his resolution.

"...The horn you employed during the entrance ceremony—what of that?" Nanao asked.

"It wouldn't be powerful enough with only three of us. And even if it was, it's a technique for playing on a living creature's instincts. I doubt it'd work on the undead."

"My double-incantation spell wouldn't be able to wipe out the entire enemy force, either," Chela added. "Direct intervention doesn't seem fruitful for us. If we just need to slow the cavalry down, then what about changing the terrain?"

"I see what you're saying, but walls created with barrier magic would be too weak. We don't have enough time to build one long enough, either."

If the wall wasn't strong enough, the enemy would burst through; if it wasn't long enough, they'd just swing around it. It would be tough time-wise to accomplish even one of those goals, but the trio needed to accomplish both. There wasn't much time left to think. The surviving allied cavalry was dwindling by the second.

"'It is a fool's game to do battle on an open field; cavalry must be fought in the forest.' I don't know if it's helpful in this situation, but my father used to say that quite a lot," Nanao muttered. The instant Oliver heard this, a single idea jumped into his mind.

"The forest—that's right! Trees!"

He simultaneously reached into his bag and grabbed the pouch full of toolplant seeds, then flashed Chela a look. She instantly understood and opened her bag for a similar pouch.

"Chela, you know what to do, right?"

"Yes! Let's use delayed casts!"

"Exactly one hundred seconds! Nanao, wait here!" Oliver shouted; then he and Chela shot off in opposite directions. They scattered the seeds from their pouches onto the ground, then drew their athames and cast a spell.

""Brogoroccio!""

They set off again, scattering more seeds, and cast the spell once more. Oliver and Chela continued this pattern over and over, running for fifty yards in opposite directions. Oliver glanced up to see their own cavalry defeated and the enemy returning in vertical lines. Based on their distance, they had about ten seconds left.

"Please work! Brogoroccio!"

Oliver cast his final spell just as Chela finished her work. Suddenly, trees began to sprout all along the straight line they'd run. The stalks arced as they grew, shooting back into the ground; eventually they connected, forming a hundred-yard-long temporary fence.

The enemy cavalry couldn't react to the sudden obstacle that appeared in their path. With no time to slow the charge of their horses, the lead troops crashed into the toolplant fence, falling to pieces and scattering countless bones everywhere. These tripped up the following cavalry, leading them to the same fate. Chela whooped for joy as she witnessed the results.

"We just barely made it…! It was a success, Oliver!"

Oliver, unable to contain his excitement as well, pumped his fist in the air. This was all thanks to Guy. His toolplants were excellent for both their ease of use and their low mana requirement. A mage needed only to imbue them with a little mana to kick-start the seeds into absorbing nutrients from the soil. This required the soil to be rich, of course, but as long as it was, the user could create a much sturdier wall than with barrier magic.

The landscape had appeared ravaged at first glance, but this was due to the skeletal warriors suddenly bursting out of the ground. That didn't mean the soil itself was devoid of nutrients. And with how verdant the second layer was, it was a good guess that there was plenty of latent fertility in this area, too. Plus, Guy's toolplants had proven reliable in their earlier battle with the chimera. With all that in mind, it wasn't a reckless gamble at all.

"Nice! Let's go, Nanao! Target the enemy general before the cavalry returns—"

The impending disaster averted for now, Oliver spun around to launch a counterattack. But Nanao was nowhere to be seen.

History was changed for the skeletal battle the moment the Rumoan cavalry failed to charge through the Kurtogan army's back. Kurtoga, which always held the advantage in pure skill of their footmen, was winning. As a result, Rumoa's imperial guards were forced to join the battle in order to push back their enemy's offense.

"—?"

The undead general stopped and surveyed its surroundings, sensing something. The skirmish had devolved into a brawl, devoid of tactics. Their battle lines were frayed in places, and it was only a matter of time before the enemy's troops spilled over to where the general was. So, with zero hesitation, the general focused on the sword in its grip.

"I have come for thy head," someone called in a dignified voice.

Severed at the torso, the general's guards toppled over, and a sword-wielding girl leaped through the resulting gap. The general's skull fell to the ground and rolled to the girl's feet. Its eyeless sockets stared at her back.

Suddenly, a voice spoke to her:

"Well done. If only we could have met when I yet had flesh, little hero."

The moment Nanao accepted this praise, the skeletal warriors across the entire battlefield crumbled. With hollow, clattering sounds, they collapsed into a giant pile of white bones. The undead were dead once again, and Chela lowered her athame in a daze.

"...I-is it...over?" she asked.

Oliver stood there, astounded as well.

Nanao sheathed her sword, then jogged over to them. "My apologies, Oliver. I saw a gap in the enemy's defenses and took my chances."

"......"

She apologized before he could say a thing. He stared at her face for a moment, then silently pinched her cheeks.

"Hyeek!"

"...I have every faith in your instincts. Still—it wouldn't have hurt to wait until we'd all grouped up."

Nanao listened to his halting speech without trying to resist his pinching. Eventually, he let go, grabbing her shoulders tightly instead. His concern was palpable.

"Please, Nanao, don't leap into danger on your own. Your safety is a thousand—a *million* times more important than winning."

"Oliver…"

She stared back into his eyes, absorbing his every word. Chela ran over, and Miligan began applauding them.

"Congrats on clearing the second layer. It's a rare feat for three first-years to accomplish, especially on their first try. You kids really are amazing."

Oliver let go of Nanao, and they turned to face Miligan.

Chela looked at the pile of bones. "…What *were* those spartoi?"

"Who knows? Necromancy isn't my expertise, so I can't say. I have zero clue why they keep re-creating that ancient battle over and over. Mr. Rivermoore might know something, though."

Miligan seemed unconcerned. A second later, an eerie smile crept onto her face.

"But if I leave it to my imagination—you never know. It could be the real generals."

A chill ran down Oliver's spine. Even after their flesh had rotted and they were only bones, the two ancient generals still sought to settle the score with their rival and continued leading armies of the dead for all eternity. If Miligan was right—then there would be no end.

"You must be tired," said Miligan. "There's a relatively safe camping ground up ahead. We've been marching hard, so we can take a long break up there."

As Miligan walked off, exhaustion set in all over Oliver's body. The echoes of victory lingering in their minds, they followed the witch in search of rest.

They found a cave positioned between the second and third layers, and here they had their first significant break since entering the labyrinth. They set up a fire in the middle of camp, boiled water, and made tea.

Miligan also put out the fruit she'd gathered while wandering the second layer. Everyone was too tired to talk much.

"Those two passed out quickly. They look so cute when they're asleep," Miligan mumbled, gazing at Nanao and Chela asleep side by side. Across the fire from her, sleep failed to grip Oliver. He watched the flames silently.

"You should rest, too, Oliver," Miligan said gently. "We took the straightest route through the second layer, but we'll have to search the entire third layer for Ophelia's workshop. You won't last long if you don't sleep now."

"...Right. Maybe after I watch the fire a little longer."

He continued to stare into the flames. Oliver knew he should sleep as soon as possible, but his eyes wouldn't close. After narrowly escaping death, his body wouldn't accept rest.

"Too nervous, huh? I understand. Here, have another cup of herbal tea."

"...Thank you."

Oliver didn't look up, feeling guilty about causing her concern. Miligan selected some herbs for their calming qualities, blended them together, and poured hot water over the leaves.

"By the way," she began, "can I ask a question?"

"...What is it? You don't need permission to ask."

"This might sound rude, but you all met upon starting at Kimberly. And you've known Pete the least amount of time, right?"

Oliver nodded.

Miligan watched the leaves unfurl inside the pot and continued softly. "So maybe I should've asked before we came down here, but... why go this far? I'm not saying you have to completely give up on him, but you could've left it all to President Godfrey and the others. If they couldn't save him, no one would have blamed you."

"......"

"Reversi are rare, to be sure, but that's no reason to risk your life, in my opinion. So why are you all so desperate to save Pete?"

An awkward smile rose on Oliver's lips. Rossi had asked him the same thing not too long ago.

"…You remember the incident at the entrance ceremony, right? Of course you do."

"Right. I'd never forget about that troll going rampant after I messed with its brain."

"That was where it all began for us—when the five of us worked together to save Katie from being smooshed by that troll."

"Hmm."

"Out of our group, Pete was the only one born to nonmagicals. He had a magic textbook for beginners tucked under his arm, and he did his best to keep from collapsing under the pressure of his new environment. He must've been more nervous than all of us combined. He'd only just realized he was a mage and was about to attend Kimberly of all places."

As he spoke, Oliver reflected thoroughly on his memories of that time. He'd never expected Pete to lend a hand. He didn't have a reason to. To Pete, they were just a bunch of noisy strangers standing next to him in line.

"But Pete didn't run. He should've been the most afraid when Marco attacked. No one would have blamed him for running away like the other new students, but he stood his ground and fought with us."

It was surely an act of the purest intentions, with no ulterior motives—driven by the inability to abandon someone in danger. In most mages, this was the first emotion that burned out.

"It made me so happy—and I'll bet the same goes for the other four—that we made such a wonderful friend on our first day at a place as awful as Kimberly."

Oliver continued staring at the fire as he revealed his honest feelings. Miligan crossed her arms.

"So you all won't run away, either, huh? …Well, isn't that beautiful."

"Are you being sarcastic?"

"Not at all. It's just quite rare. Honestly, it's 'outside' logic. Basically a fairy tale here at Kimberly. But I don't mind it. Kind of gives me the warm fuzzies." Grinning, Miligan reached for the pot on the campfire. The tea leaves had completely unfurled during their chat. "Speaking of odd ducks...I'm most surprised by you."

"...?" Oliver was confused by the change of direction in their conversation.

"With a bit of effort," Miligan continued, "I can understand Chela and Nanao. Everything about them, from their innate talents to the environments they were raised in, is extraordinary. A half-elf McFarlane and a samurai from an island to the Far East. This might sound contradictory, but the way they exceed expectations is an expectation in and of itself. But what about you? I don't know anything about your background, although"—the witch looked up at Oliver as she poured the steaming red liquid into a cup—"at the very least, I can say you're intrinsically ordinary compared to those two. Your mana levels and spell power are all average among first-years, and it doesn't seem to me that you excel in any particular field. If you asked ten people, I'm sure they'd all describe you the same way: a jack-of-all-trades, master of none destined for average success at best."

"......"

"But here you are, fighting side by side with those two. And from what I've seen, you can hold your own. That, plus the fact that you're still a first-year—it's truly mysterious, you know?"

She handed him the cup of tea, which he accepted without a word. His silence didn't seem to bother her.

"Chela and Nanao were trained body and mind in the perfect environments for their respective exceptional talents. It's unheard of for those not similarly blessed to stand in the same arena at the same age—impossible, really. Do you understand what I'm saying? The fact that you're here, now, can only be called magic."

Oliver sipped his tea in lieu of responding. The witch understood that there was nothing *to* say.

"You could answer, *'I worked my ass off to make up for a lack of talent'*—but it would mean nothing. It's not enough. Even if you found the most amazing teacher and dedicated your entire life so far to training, it wouldn't be nearly enough to get you this far. At least, not by any methods I'm aware of."

She studied him again with her human eye, as well as the basilisk eye peeking out from behind her bangs.

"There must be something about your past that makes even this eye of mine downright sweet by comparison."

Oliver returned her stare, fighting back against the pressure of her gaze.

Miligan laughed and clapped her hands, letting it slide off her like water. "I don't mean to pry. It's only natural for mages to have checkered pasts. As your senior, though, I can't help but be concerned. There's an element of danger about you. Katie and Nanao have it, too, but not like this."

The sudden mentor-like concern in her voice took Oliver off guard, and he looked away. He still found it difficult to tell how much of what she did was driven by kindness versus out of ulterior motives. She seemed very tolerant and caring, which made her even more difficult to deal with. He refused to rely on her too much or potentially let down his guard.

"Sorry, am I running my mouth? Have I bored you into sleep yet?"

"...I think sleep will come if I lie down," he said, trying to convince himself of this. If he didn't get to sleep soon, he would definitely perform worse tomorrow. So he chugged the last of his tea.

Miligan had a thought. "Hmm… If you're still wide awake, then maybe I can help you relax."

She stood up from the rock she'd been using as a seat, walked over to Oliver, and got behind him. As she slipped her arms around his shoulders, she whispered in his ear.

"...Or are you not into naughty things?"

"—!"

Oliver instantly pushed her arms away and stood up. He slapped his empty teacup onto the stone he'd been sitting on, then walked briskly to the other side of the fire and silently lay down, his back to the witch. He couldn't have done more to say "no" even if he tried. Miligan grinned in self-derision, her hand still stinging from his rejection.

"Not a fan of those jokes, huh? Forgive me. It's in a mage's instincts to try and seduce those who pique their curiosity. Good night, Oliver. Sweet dreams."

Her voice was as soft as ever. Oliver squeezed his eyes shut tightly in an effort to drive her existence out of his mind, forcing himself to sleep.

After their first interaction in earnest, things between them began to change gradually.

"...Um..."

"Oh, Ophelia! Excellent, you're here. Sit!"

It had been a long time since she'd entered the Fellowship during the evening. The surrounding students stared unpleasantly at her, but unlike before, she now had a table welcoming her. Encouraged by Godfrey's booming voice, she sat down.

"Let me introduce you to my friends. They might seem thorny at first, but once you get past that, you'll see they're all good folks."

There were two other students at the table besides Godfrey and Carlos. One was a small, dainty first-year boy, and the other was a second-year girl with locks and a sharp air about her. The boy appeared to be from the Union, but the girl's dark skin and facial features suggested she likely had roots in another continent. It was rare to see people with foreign ancestry at Kimberly.

"...I'll concede that we've formed a bond, however unintentional. But we are definitely not friends."

"I certainly don't remember befriending you."

The boy and girl quickly contradicted him, then glared furiously at each other.

Ophelia stiffened at the unexpectedly standoffish reception; Godfrey noticed this and intervened.

"Hey now, you're scaring her. Save the fighting for later. Introduce yourselves, and don't interrupt."

They reluctantly ceased their staring contest and turned to the new girl to introduce themselves.

"I'm Lesedi Ingwe, a second-year. Call on me whenever you want."

"Tim Linton, first-year. Feel free not to remember it."

Their introductions were quite blunt. Ophelia cautiously introduced herself as well and was surprised to see them barely react to the name Salvadori.

Godfrey nodded in satisfaction. "The four of us are sort of like the academy's neighborhood watch. Of course, we're only second-years and still finding our footing, but this place is just too dangerous. Our goal is to spread effective methods of self-defense while helping as many students as we can who get caught up in unwanted trouble or are possibly about to be."

"Help...people?"

Ophelia ruminated on the unfamiliar words. Godfrey seemed accustomed to this reaction and shrugged dryly. "I won't deny that most people think we're strange. But it's a wide world, with varied interests. You can always count on us for help, of course—and if you'd be so kind as to join us, why, nothing would make me happier." He looked her straight in the eye as he cut to the chase.

"...That said," Carlos added, "we've basically completely failed to lure in any younger students. Anyone with any interest quits before long."

"No, no! I'm still here, Carlos!" Tim's hand shot into the air.

Carlos winced a little. "I appreciate it. But unfortunately, it seems you're sixty percent of the reason most new recruits quit."

"I demand perfection, is all! We don't need any halfhearted comrades."

"Love the enthusiasm. But what's the truth?"

"Mr. Godfrey's attention should be on me and me alone! Everyone else can just die!"

His honesty was refreshing, although Lesedi held her head with a grimace.

Ophelia looked at them all in turn, swallowed nervously, then cautiously opened her mouth.

"...Can I really be of help?" she asked.

Tim and Lesedi appeared surprised, as if they hadn't expected her to react that way after seeing the previous interaction.

Lesedi straightened up a bit and looked at Ophelia. "Let me ask this instead: What do you bring to the table?"

"Huh?"

Ophelia was at a loss for words. It was her first time joining a group, and thus also the first time someone was asking something of her. As her mind went blank, Carlos swooped in to assist.

"Don't worry—she brings a lot. Lia's a hard worker."

Her childhood friend flashed her a grin, and Ophelia felt a little calmer. She reviewed the things she'd just heard and came up with a list they might require.

"...Um, if it's healing magic or simple potions, maybe..."

The moment she heard this, Lesedi slammed her hands on the table and leaned forward. "Can you heal burns?"

"Huh? Y-yes..."

"What about acid burns? Poisoning?"

"...? I-it would depend on the severity, but for most cases..."

The oddly specific examples made Ophelia hesitate as she answered based on her skills. Lesedi jumped out of her chair and grabbed her by the shoulders.

"I'm not letting you get away, newbie."

"Hwuh...?"

"Lemme tell ya... One of the people at this table has a cannon for a wand and is more likely to hit friendlies than enemies. Another is obsessed with poisoning but doesn't know how to make antidotes for his own concoctions," Lesedi said irritably and shot the others a piercing look.

Godfrey and Tim jumped to defend themselves.

"Hold on, now! I haven't been *that* bad lately!"

"Neither have I! I've been avoiding any aerosolized poisons, haven't I? And you know how much I love their potential for mass murder!"

"Shut up, you idiots! How many times do you think I've nearly died thanks to you two?"

Ophelia watched them argue in a daze; it all made sense now: The specific questions of burns, acid, and poison came from personal experience with them. She'd sensed that what they did was dangerous, but she hadn't expected anything like this.

"U-um…"

"Please, you have to help me! I'm no good at healing, and Carlos can't keep up with them alone!"

Lesedi grabbed her hand, practically begging now. This was Ophelia's first time experiencing such strong desire for her skills—so of course, she didn't know how to refuse.

After joining the neighborhood watch, Ophelia learned a lot about her new friends. As she'd expected, they all had a quirk or two—but what left the deepest impression was Alvin Godfrey's extreme clumsiness.

"Flamma!"

They'd secured an empty classroom for training purposes, and for some reason, Godfrey took off his robe and rolled up his sleeves in order to demonstrate his magic for her. A blindingly powerful fireball exploded from the tip of his wand—and set his wand hand on fire.

"Guh…!"

"Oh no!"

Ophelia immediately extinguished it with a spell. The smell of burning flesh filled the room, and Godfrey sighed.

"I'm fine... And thanks for the help."

Ophelia stared in awe at his arm, terribly burned from elbow to tip. At the same time, she realized why he'd taken off his robe and rolled up his sleeve: He'd known this would happen.

"Ever since I first learned this spell, it always turns out like this. I'm unable to control it, so not only is the output unstable, but it also shoots back into my own arm. According to Instructor Gilchrist, I'm not able to properly control my innate mana supply. I've gotten a little better over time, though," he explained with a bitter expression, as if the pain of his burns was nothing compared to his inability to control his magic.

"I've been relying on Carlos to heal me, but it seems I'll be relying on you, too, from now on... Pathetic, isn't it? If only I could use healing magic myself and not waste so much of everyone's effort..."

"...D-don't worry about it."

Ophelia carefully chose her words, then pointed her wand at Godfrey's arm. This wasn't something that could be fixed in a day, and the fine mana control of healing magic would be beyond him. In that case...

"Whenever you're burned...I'll be there. I'll heal you...right up."

She'd accept that role, she decided, and began treating his burn.

✽

"...That was three years ago, huh? How time flies," Carlos muttered, reflecting on old memories as they trudged through the dusky marsh. Godfrey quickly knew what exactly they were referring to.

"When Ophelia was still with us, eh? ...I was all spirit, no substance. I jumped into everything feetfirst without thinking... Just remembering those days is embarrassing."

"That spirit is what attracted people to you. Those are fond memories."

Carlos smiled at him—but bitter regret clouded Godfrey's face.

"...Unfortunately, I messed up. That's why she left. Why this is happening."

"That wasn't your fault."

Carlos shook their head and tried to deny it, but Godfrey wouldn't accept it. He wasn't so conceited as to think he might have been able to do something. He was aware of his own clumsiness, especially back then. But even so, he couldn't help himself.

"Still, I should have done something... I was her mentor."

✳

Meanwhile, up on the surface beneath the noon sun, Katie and Guy waited for their friends to return.

"...Oh, you want to help me? Thank you, Milihand."

The two of them were holed up in a corner of the lounge, making copies of their morning class notes for their friends. They also had a very helpful assistant who would turn the page just as they were done copying the text: Miligan's hand, severed by Nanao, then given artificial life and repurposed as a familiar by Miligan. Better known as Milihand.

Katie stroked its back—its knuckles, actually—and praised it, which elicited shocked spit takes from the students passing by.

"...I can't believe you," Guy said exasperatedly. "That's Miligan's severed hand, y'know."

"I'm aware, but...it's quite charming. It really seems to like me."

And indeed, Milihand was all over Katie's arm like a cat. The process of turning it into a familiar meant a lot of its behavior was artificial, but still, Milihand seemed quite expressive. It could manipulate the muscles on its palm around the eye, creating all sorts of "expressions." Guy watched apprehensively as Milihand strolled happily over the table.

He sighed deeply. "...You think Oliver's gonna be okay?"

"I have faith… They promised they'd all come back alive," Katie said firmly, continuing to copy her notes. The tall boy shook his head.

"I know what they said…but he's a guy. The only one."

She looked at him, confused for a moment. "What about it?"

"*Sigh*… What, did you forget they're up against Ophelia Salvadori? I haven't seen its effects myself, but she's got that powerful Perfume of hers going twenty-four seven, right? Spend enough time in it, and… well, it'll be easy to get a *rise* out of him," Guy answered awkwardly, looking away.

After a few moments of silence, Katie jumped up, her face flushed. "Wh-what the heck? What are you suggesting?!"

"I'm just saying…it's, uh…*hard* not to be concerned…"

"O-Oliver would never!"

"Easy for you to say. It ain't so easy for us when there's that much pressure," Guy grumbled, placing his hands on his cheeks.

Katie, who had apparently not considered this angle at all, suddenly panicked.

"Then again, Chela seems like she'd be wise in that regard…," Guy added. "Plus, they have Miligan, so maybe there's no point in me worrying."

"W-wise?! What's that supposed to mean? What's Ms. Miligan going to do?! Tell meee!!"

Katie rushed up to him, grabbed his shoulders, and shook him. Just then, a student pushing a large wagon full of items for sale passed by.

"Extra, extra! Today's headline: 'Revelation! Kimberly's Sex Life'!"

"Gimme one!"

"One, please!"

The two of them instantly placed an order. They'd never once read the gossip column before, but today they pored over it with intense scrutiny.

*

As they entered the third layer, the labyrinth once again changed completely. The verdant, earthy smell from the previous layer was almost gone, replaced by muddy soil that gave off an unpleasant dampness. One wrong step would see you sink in to your ankles; in places, it was even a bottomless swamp. The artificial sun on the second layer kept things eternally bright, but here the only light source was the luminous moss covering the ceiling. As a result, the entire layer was dim. Many magical creatures suitable to a swamp also resided here, requiring extreme caution from all who would venture into its depths.

"*Huff! Huff...!*"

"*Wheeze...!*"

The chimera collapsed into the mud with a loud *thud*. Oliver's group looked at the recently slain giant and breathed a sigh of relief—far worse than their environment was the fact that they were now encountering many more chimeras than previously. They'd analyzed their opponent, discovered its weakness, and efficiently brought it down, all while struggling against their terrible footing. After only three hours in the third layer, they'd repeated this process four times already. If you included the instances when they'd avoided a fight thanks to early scouting, then their chimera encounter numbers skyrocketed.

"Hmm, so this is the fourth one? We should have expected many more chimera on the third layer. Let's keep moving."

Miligan urged them on, and Oliver resumed trudging through the sludge. The Azian girl came jogging up behind him.

"That was excellent coordination, Oliver!"

"...Yeah."

Nanao enthusiastically slung an arm around his shoulder, not particularly bothered by the tricky terrain. The break they'd taken before exiting the second layer must have done wonders for her, because she was even more energetic than before. Which was a good thing. A very good thing—but Oliver had a different problem. After struggling with it for a bit, he quietly asked, "...Nanao, could you try to be less handsy?"

"Huh?"

She froze on the spot, then took a few shaky steps backward in the mud and turned to Chela with tears in her eyes.

"…Oliver hates meee…"

"No!" he hurried to say.

Chela, seeing the truth, intervened. "That's right. He doesn't hate you, Nanao. The Perfume has just gotten too hard to bear. Right, Oliver?"

She'd noticed it not too long ago.

The boy averted his eyes in shame, then nodded bitterly. "I hate to admit it, but yes… Ever since we entered the third layer, it's been getting thicker with each step. Of course, I'd never let it take over my mind—but in our situation, I'd rather not lose focus," Oliver said with a sigh. It was true—ever since he set foot in this layer, the girls' skin had looked dangerously enticing; their every movement drew in his eyes. Without a doubt, it was because the air was thick with Perfume.

Normally, he could handle it by honing his self-control. But when a girl came into close contact with him like earlier, things got stickier. There was no telling when he might slip, distracted by their touch, and do something he'd regret. This was especially true with Nanao, who had a tendency to ignore personal space. But the girl seemed mystified, and she cocked her head at him.

"? How is it hard, Oliver?"

"Nanao, please, that's not…"

"He's pitching a tent," Miligan said, getting straight to the point. "It's to be expected, though. The Perfume has that effect."

Oliver frowned, but Nanao crossed her arms in confusion. "…Pitching a tent? What does that mean…?"

"Don't dwell on it, Nanao. I'm good now. You don't need to intervene, Ms. Miligan."

He focused on his breathing, ironing out his Perfume-addled thoughts.

Miligan eyed him. "Hmm… You do seem to be resisting it fine, but if it gets to be too much, don't hesitate to speak up. We've got a long way to go. You won't be able to force yourself forever."

"I can handle this on my own. Like I said, your assistance isn't needed," he stated flatly and set off once more, practically emanating his rejection of Miligan's offer.

The witch grinned wryly. "He's stubborn. Guess I touched a nerve again."

"...What did you do while we were asleep?" Chela asked.

"Just gave him a little sexual invitation."

"He's a first-year! What were you thinking?!"

Chela rounded on her, unable to overlook this despite being outranked. Meanwhile, Nanao cautiously approached Oliver as he continued forward.

"...Is this far enough, Oliver?"

"Yeah, that's good. Sorry about the inconvenience."

Unlike before, Nanao was now about an arm's length away from him. However, this seemed to perturb her as she raised and lowered her hand restlessly. It bothered her to be unable to engage like they did previously.

"...This is frustrating."

"No, this is normal. You're the one who's way too touchy-feely."

"So you *do* hate it?"

"I never said that," Oliver firmly replied, and Nanao continued to walk alongside him at that strange middling distance. Miligan, tuning out Chela's lecture, watched the awkward scene play out. She covered one eye with her hand.

"...How to describe it? They're so bright, it's like my eye's going to be destroyed."

"If you really think that, then please keep your bizarre flirtations to yourself and just watch from the sidelines," Chela insisted sternly, and Miligan glanced at her.

"Sure, I'm more than happy to. But are you?"

"...What is that supposed to mean?"

Chela scowled, but it wasn't long before her eyes turned to the two ahead. There was a jealousy, an admiration in her gaze, as if she was observing a line she could never cross.

"Aw, geez. You guys really make me want to get you all home safely." Miligan shrugged, then clapped her hands to get everyone's attention. "Now, we should have a discussion. At the moment, we're simply walking in the direction where the Perfume's strongest, but that won't be enough to locate Ophelia's workshop. We'll need to find some kind of clue."

Chela crossed her arms and thought. "We could tail a chimera... No, that would be useless."

"Indeed, she wouldn't leave such an obvious trail. Most of the chimeras released from her workshop are subsequently abandoned. It's also likely she won't be bringing back any more of her chimeras designed for capturing, either."

Oliver groaned. As he'd expected, finding a single workshop in the vast third layer wouldn't be an easy task. He forced himself to switch gears.

"Let's narrow the search from a different angle," he said. "If you were going to put a workshop down here, where would you start?"

He looked at Miligan, the most experienced of them all in the labyrinth. She put a hand to her chin and pondered.

"First, location's important. Naturally, the highest priority is not being found by other students or magical beasts. This layer has plenty of water, so we can exclude that from our criteria. To make gathering materials easier, I'd want to be closer to the second layer..." At this point, Miligan stopped and reconsidered. "...No, that's just my opinion. There are plenty of good spots in the fourth layer and beyond. They're too dangerous for me, but I wouldn't doubt that Ophelia could make them her main sources for materials and the like. With that in mind, it's actually a high possibility that her workshop is near the fourth layer."

Oliver recalled Miligan saying that Ophelia Salvadori outclassed her. If she had the respect of Vera Miligan, then the third layer might be no different from strolling through a garden for Ophelia.

"That will be a problem, though. We'll have to cross *this* in order to get to the fourth layer."

Miligan resumed walking, and they followed. Five minutes later, the mud had become much more watery, eventually turning into a massive wetland. The whole landscape stretched beyond what they could see, so it was impossible to judge just how massive the marsh was. The opposite shore probably lay somewhere beyond the mist. Chela looked down at the cloudy water's surface.

"...It's a swamp, isn't it? A very, very big one."

"This is the Miasma Marsh, the most perilous section of the whole layer," Miligan explained. The air stung at their throats when they inhaled, helping to explain the moniker. Poisonous gas seemed to be bubbling up from the swamp, permeating the entire area.

"At most, there are two methods for crossing the swamp: Hop on a broom and fly over or get in a boat and float. But since I have you three with me, we'll be sticking to a boat this time."

"Oh? Why is that?" Nanao asked, confused. A broom seemed like the fastest method, so it was a natural question. Miligan looked up at the oddly thick mist dozens of yards above them.

"First, because the closer you get to the ceiling, the thicker the miasma gets. Fly too high, and you'll get a full-body dose of it. That won't be a pretty sight."

"How...bad are we talking?" Chela asked.

"Your skin will melt, you'll go blind, your lungs will shut down, and your mind will turn to mush. Naturally, the miasma also negatively affects brooms, since they feed on the mana in the air. Ultimately, you'll fall into the swamp and become fish food."

Chela furrowed her brow at the grisly thought. Miligan continued: "You can mitigate the effects somewhat with enough prep, but you still have to be careful not to fly too high. You'll also have to deal with *those* things on your tail."

She looked down, and the others followed her gaze. They spotted a bunch of shadows flitting above the water's surface with long, cylindrical bodies and lacy wings. Hundreds of them dotted the marshland in large groups.

"Skyfish..."

"Yup. Low-flying magical fish that inhabit wetlands. A single one's not a big deal, but their schools are massive. Most often, you get tangled up in them and fall into the swamp. Happened to me once, too," Miligan said. The revelation of her past failure, more than any of her explanations, was most effective at grabbing their attention. As the trio considered this in silence, Miligan shared the other method they could choose.

"It might take longer, but in a boat, we can burn some incense that will keep the skyfish away. Of course, we'll still have to be wary of the beasts within the swamp. Lots of different varieties make their home in the labyrinth, so it's basically a roulette as to what we'll encounter."

The three of them lowered their gazes from the skyfish to the water's surface. It made sense that the water held its own threats—this was the labyrinth, after all. There were no completely safe paths. In the end, they had to assess the risks and choose for themselves.

"That said," Miligan continued, "between the four of us, we should be able to beat back just about anything. Thus, the boat. It'll be easier to help one another than on broomsticks, and if worse comes to worst, we can abandon the boat and fly the rest of the way."

And so Miligan made the decision for them to go by boat.

Oliver nodded; nothing of what he heard led him to argue otherwise.

"...I agree. Speed is important, but what's most important is that we all cross safely."

"I agree, too," Chela said. "What about you, Nanao?"

"I am fine with either choice. Whichever you all prefer."

With no one opposed, Oliver quickly moved on to the next step. "Good," he said. "So first, we have to make a boat. There's not much left, but we can use the rest of our toolplants to build one."

"That would speed things up," Miligan replied. "I ought to get on my knees and thank Guy when we get back."

"...I hope that's all you're doing on your knees."

"Ha-ha-ha! Don't worry. I'm not *that* desperate."

Miligan laughed off Chela's warning, and they got to building the boat. Suddenly, Oliver sensed a mana frequency coming his way.

(*...I have bad news, my lord.*) Teresa Carste, his secret scout, was contacting him.

(*What is it?*) he asked, and she immediately responded.

(*If you mean to cross by boat, then I will not be able to maintain the same distance I have so far. I have my own boat, but the swamp is too still. I must stay far away, or Snake Eye will notice me. I'm ashamed to say it, but our best option is to regroup on the other side.*)

Oliver cursed his lack of foresight. She was so good at scouting in secrecy that he hadn't spared a single thought for how the swamp might affect her. That said, there was no other choice. Oliver thought for a few seconds, then agreed.

(*All right, that's fine. I'll leave a trail when we hit the other side. Follow it back to me.*)

(*Understood. This layer is dangerous. Please be careful, my lord.*)

And with that, her presence quickly faded. Oliver had kept working the whole while, so the others didn't seem to suspect a thing. He refocused on building the boat—after ten minutes of weaving strands of toolplant together, it was done.

"Looks good to me," Miligan said, staring down at it and crossing her arms in satisfaction. It was halfway between a boat and a raft but wide enough to let all four of them walk around on it. There was a mast in the center, to which they affixed a square sail of magically reinforced cloth. For a slapdash construction, it wasn't half-bad.

"Let's set sail, then—actually, one thing first." They'd pushed the boat to the water and were ready to board when Miligan stopped them. "Since we're here, how about a lesson?"

"A lesson...?" Chela repeated. "What could we possibly do here?"

"Oh, this is the perfect spot for the Lanoff-style technique Lake Walk. Oliver, Chela, you've heard of it, yes?"

The two first-years eyed Miligan as she hopped off the boat toward the swamp. Oliver grimaced, but her feet silently landed on the water. Nanao gaped incredulously.

"...Ohhh! She's standing on the water!"

"Love that reaction. Walking on water is an important technique for mages and is said to test every facet of spatial magic basics."

As Miligan explained, she strolled across the water's surface. Gentle ripples reverberated outward from her feet, but her footing seemed rock-solid.

Oliver and Chela goggled. It was basically a perfect example of Lake Walk.

"This requires a certain amount of mana output, so normally you'd start practicing it in your second year. But from what I've seen, you three are more than capable. So why not try it out now? Go on."

She beckoned with her hand, and the three of them looked at the water.

"...Um, if we fail, we'll fall into the water," said Chela.

"Should sharpen your focus, right? Don't want to fall into the swamp teeming with monsters." Miligan grinned. She wanted them to turn the risk into motivation.

"Hrm. Then I shall start."

While Oliver and Chela took a few seconds to prepare themselves, Nanao immediately strode forth onto the water. Before they could react, her foot hit the surface—and she plunged straight into the marsh.

"Mmgh...!"

"Ha-ha-ha! You really sank like a stone. You okay?"

Miligan extended a hand and dragged her back onto land. Nanao shook her head, soaked. "What a conundrum. I haven't the faintest idea how to do it."

"It shouldn't be that difficult once you grasp the essentials. Oliver, your turn."

The boy looked at the water, then breathed out. *Calm down. You can do this. You've practiced earth stance so many times. This is just the same.*

"...!"

Steeling himself, he took a step. The tip of his toe touched the water and seemed to sink, but it was pushed back by the water before it could. He followed up with his left foot. He expelled mana into the water's surface, just like he did with Grave Step, all the while careful not to focus his weight on one foot more than the other. Shakily, he stood on two feet on the rippling water.

"Whoa!"

"Yes, yes! I knew you could do it, since you mastered earth stance so well. Okay, now try walking."

Oliver didn't hesitate this time. He replicated the sensation again while it was fresh in his mind and walked across the water with few ripples. Of course, this was far more tiring than simply walking on land. Ten minutes of this would have him on the brink of exhaustion. Chela studied his movements in wonder. He wasn't as effortless as Miligan, but he was indeed walking on water.

"Fantastic," Miligan said. "By distributing your weight as you walk and economizing your mana output, you can make the water support your body. It's very impressive that you can do this on your first try."

"......"

"This is a necessary step in learning the more advanced technique, Sky Walk. As a mage, and as a sword arts practitioner, you've taken a huge step forward, Oliver."

The witch praised him with surprising enthusiasm. It surfaced a memory buried deep within the confines of Oliver's mind.

"Neat, huh? Don't worry—I'm sure you'll be able to do it, too, Noll. You're my son, after all."

*   *   *

As a young boy, the idea of standing in midair was the greatest thing ever. And, unaware of how lofty a goal it was, he swore to himself to one day reach those same heights—still totally ignorant of what the word *talent* meant. He closed his eyes and thought, *I'm making progress on that goal.*

"…Nanao. You come, too."

Before he realized it, he'd reached out his hand toward his friend. There was no deep thought behind the gesture. He simply believed without a doubt that she could stand in the same place, by his side.

"…Right!"

And Nanao jumped at the offer. Her eyes on his extended hand, she once again launched herself onto the water—and shakily landed without sinking or splashing.

"Oh? Ohhh? …I did it!"

Her feet firm on the water, Nanao grabbed Oliver's hand tightly and shouted. Miligan's eyes went wide.

"Goodness, so you did. Did Oliver's example show you the key? Or…was it purely your desire to stand next to him?" she teased, then glanced over at Chela, standing alone on the bank while her friends celebrated.

"……"

Of course, Chela wasn't one to wallow. She closed her eyes, shook off the nerves and pressure, then opened her eyes again and stepped onto the water. The three of them watched as her right foot touched the surface—and her left foot immediately followed after.

"…Whew. I'm here, too!"

"Ohhh, Chela! You made it!"

"Never doubted you for a second."

The three of them, united on the water, clasped hands and rejoiced. Miligan smiled and nodded.

"Thankfully, you all managed just fine. If anyone falls out of the boat, you'll be able to survive. Now, let's set sail!"

Once everyone was in the boat, the witch cast a spell on the sail. A sudden gust began blowing, and the vessel slipped out onto the water.

As they sailed, Miligan explained to the three of them how she was managing it.

"A yacht isn't as versatile as a broomstick, but it's still a useful ride for a mage. Nonmagicals need to adjust the sail while studying the wind, but for us—"

She pointed her athame at the sail, indicating the magical circle and text upon it. This was the reason they were moving without oars or paddles. Oliver had heard of seafaring mages who employed these techniques, but he'd never seen them in person.

"—we can summon wind elementals and place them around the sail. It's a little tricky, but once you've got it, you can keep moving without lifting a finger. You'd do well to remember this."

"I see... That's very educational."

Chela listened with rapt attention. Oliver looked over and saw Nanao stooped on the side of the boat. Black shadows raced beneath the water's murky surface.

"...Those are some big fish."

"Be careful, Nanao," Oliver warned. "They could attack at any moment."

"Mm... Still, they might be tasty grilled with a bit of salt."

"You're hungry now?!"

Nanao never changed, even this deep into the labyrinth. It was at once aggravating and reassuring. Suddenly, Oliver noticed a shift in the atmosphere and closed his mouth. He looked around to see the others listening intently as well.

"...They've all disappeared," Chela remarked.

"Yeah. That's a bit odd," Miligan replied, nodding. Not only were the fish under the water gone, but the skyfish weren't even hovering near the edges of the incense. They were supposed to look out for attacks from below on this route, yet there was no sign of any danger.

"It's actually quite unnatural to get this far unscathed. Plus, it's too quiet. Maybe there's something odd happening deep below—"

Miligan scanned wide about them, and out of the corner of her eye, she spotted the flash of a white figure.

"? Was there something out there…?"

"……"

The witch was silent, and Chela, who'd apparently seen the same thing, furrowed her brow. A terrible feeling came over Oliver, and he reached for the athame at his waist. Suddenly, the boat began listing.

"Whoa…?!"

His body pitched forward, so he grabbed on to the mast to stabilize himself. The boat had accelerated without warning, shooting across the water.

"What are you doing?!" Chela shouted at their captain, Miligan. "Why are we going so fast?"

"That thing's bad news! Everyone, athames at the ready!" Miligan barked, and the three of them drew. Instantly, the water behind the boat rose and burst. From the spray appeared a sea serpent at least twenty yards in length—or its skeleton, at least. It was completely devoid of flesh, like a museum display. It shouldn't have been capable of moving, yet it slithered after them with incredible vivacity.

"Wha—?!"

"Mmgh, more bones?"

"A sea serpent…! Salvadori's *other* familiar! You three, hold on tight!"

Heeding her warning, they dropped low. Miligan blasted the sail with a spell, exciting the wind elementals. The boat instantly reached over double its original speed, beginning an aquatic game of chase with the serpent.

"That thing's far more dangerous than any chimera, so it's time to make a run for it! It shouldn't be able to catch us on land!"

"I agree, but can we go fast enough with this boat?!" Chela yelled.

"If we get caught, we'll cross that bridge when we come to it! Get your brooms ready!" Miligan shouted; Oliver and Chela nodded at each other, then turned toward the skeletal serpent chasing them and unleashed a volley of spells. This seemed to be quite effective, as the creature began to slow down, and the distance between them widened.

"Good thing we put some effort into this craft! Looks like we'll escape by the skin of our teeth!"

The witch laughed triumphantly—but a few seconds later, her smile stiffened like stone.

"...Uh, this might be bad."

"Huh?"

Oliver swung around to look ahead of them. Numerous bones were floating in the boat's path, like the remains of some great creature's meal—at least, that's what it appeared to be at first glance.

"Congreganta."

That one incantation revealed its true identity. Before their very eyes, the bones began re-forming—first, a spinal column the size of a great tree, to which a skull connected; simultaneously, ribs and fins materialized. A giant, coiled sea serpent, much like the one chasing them, now blocked their path.

"Wha—?"

"Guh—!"

Realizing they were going to crash, Miligan pulled hard to port. The boat nearly screeched at the sudden force, and they sailed in an arc just before hitting the serpent, kicking up white froth. They'd avoided immediate disaster, but the maneuver had also lost them a lot of speed.

"Yeesh...! Thanks for the surprise greeting, Rivermoore!"

Miligan glared ahead as she kneeled on the deck, and the others turned to see what she was looking at. On the other side of the serpent, through the gaps in its ribs, they could see him.

"Oh, but *I'm* the one who's surprised here."

The mage was standing on a giant turtle shell like a boat, with the austerity of a wicked priest as he studied the four of them with dark eyes. Not only did he give off the characteristically overwhelming force of someone far stronger than them, but an aura of death also clung to his entire body.

"What exactly are you doing, bringing three pieces of young meat with you to the land of death, Snake Eye?"

Oliver and Chela shivered in fright—they'd encountered this man in the labyrinth once before. Cyrus Rivermoore—a necromancer who used special techniques to control the dead, and equally as dangerous as Ophelia Salvadori.

"Ophelia kidnapped their friend. We're going to rescue him," Miligan answered, unbothered.

He chuckled in his throat. "Sounds like a complicated way to kill yourself."

"I don't blame you for seeing it that way, but we're actually hoping to get home alive." The witch shrugged.

Rivermoore snorted in derision. "You intend to survive a fight with Salvadori in her current state? I thought you were smarter than that."

"Touché." Miligan grinned bitterly, unable to argue with him. But it was at this moment, when there was a lull in the conversation, that someone decided to interject.

"Forgive my intrusion, Mr. Rivermoore, but are you perhaps also searching for Ophelia Salvadori's workshop?"

"Chela?!"

Oliver stared at her in disbelief.

Rivermoore turned his dusky gaze toward the unexpected questioner. "...Why do you ask me that, McFarlane girl?"

"Because I thought it was a possibility. You must be after *something* if you're down on the third layer at a time like this. And there aren't that many reasons a Kimberly student would voluntarily get near another who's been consumed by the spell."

"……"

"The first reason would be that someone important has been taken, like in our case. Many students are assisting in this endeavor, but I doubt you're one of them. The second reason would be if one were interested in the consumed student's magic."

She boldly made her claim in the face of a man much more powerful than she was. Oliver could tell that this wasn't just a reckless, ignorant gamble on Chela's part—from his position next to her, he could see her hands quivering. She knew all too well that the man before them was at least Ophelia Salvadori's equal and could wipe them all out if he felt like it. But he also could hold a clue to saving Pete.

"The latter seems to fit you perfectly," Chela continued. "More specifically, I believe you want to seize Ophelia Salvadori's magical research before anyone else can get the chance. That's why you're here, isn't it?"

Oliver swallowed. She had a point—if this was the case, then their goals didn't clash. All they wanted was to rescue Pete, so if they were able to do that, then they'd leave Ophelia's research alone.

"If I'm right, then why don't we work together? Three of us may be first-years, but we have the numbers. If we share our information and search together, we'll have much better odds of finding the workshop. Even you could see some value in that."

Finally, she made her proposal. Even if they did manage to safely reach the bank, there was still no guarantee they'd find Ophelia's workshop—all the more reason why Chela was attempting to negotiate with this sorcerer. By emphasizing they weren't enemies, she might be able to draw out a little information from him.

Everyone held their breaths in silence. Rivermoore studied Chela for a while, then shook his head.

"I wish I could say it was an excellent suggestion…but unfortunately, you missed the mark."

"…What?"

"I have no fixation on Salvadori's research. Our goals as mages are far too different. Even if I did get my hands on her work, it would serve me no purpose...though I won't reject it if it falls into my lap. But that's not a good enough reason for me to risk my own neck."

Chela wasn't deterred by his unexpected response. He *had* to have a good reason for being down here.

"...Then why are you here? Is there another reason to place yourself in danger unrelated to her research?" she asked.

Rivermoore's lips curled in a dry smile. "A reason, eh? ...Yes, that is a good question."

He wasn't belittling Chela, but himself. At the same time, they now had definitive proof that he wasn't here for personal gain.

"...Don't tell me you're her Final Visitor?" Miligan asked softly.

Rivermoore snorted at the notion. "Don't be a fool. I wouldn't be invited here for something like that. Although...I suppose you could entrust me to express my condolences to the family. A funeral with only the deceased and a single mourner is a sad affair indeed."

He spoke with a touch of humility, yet seemed entirely uninterested in helping them understand. With a bit of resignation, Rivermoore turned back to Chela.

"We've tried to kill each other more times than I have fingers to count. It's the least I can do for my junior... Is that enough of an answer, McFarlane?"

"......"

Chela had prepared for the worst but found herself unable to press further. Similar goals, mutually beneficial—even attempting a discussion with such ordinary measures seemed likely to only expose her ignorance.

"Are you done stalling for time? Then let us continue."

At his command, the two sea serpents raised their heads. Chela, seeing her negotiation had failed, readied her athame reluctantly.

"...So it must come to this after all?"

"No. You did well, Chela," Miligan said with a triumphant smile.

Oliver looked at her quizzically. Then he noticed—she'd been on her knees the whole time they were talking to Rivermoore.

"I can understand the duty one feels to one's juniors. But for a simple condolence call, the venue you chose is a bit much. Don't you agree, Rivermoore?"

Oliver gasped as he realized. Miligan was kneeling on the boat's deck, creating a blind spot around her feet with her robe—where she'd squeezed her athame through a gap in the construction. The tip of her blade was in contact with the water, injecting something into the swamp.

A wave surged from one side of the boat, causing it to shake. The water had been totally calm during their voyage, so Oliver knew that there couldn't be waves without *something* creating them.

"...Tch."

Rivermoore realized the witch's plan a second too late. The sound had hardly left his mouth before dozens of tentacles burst out of the water around him.

The sea serpents quickly moved to get between the threat and their master, and the tentacles wrapped around their bony bodies before two giant, slimy masses emerged from the water. The creature was the size of a small island, with a bizarre mix of squid and octopus characteristics. The first-years stared at the monster in horror.

"An aquatic chimera...!"

"I knew it! I knew Salvadori, the author of *A Study of Rapid Development from Interbreeding Krakens and Scyllas*, would leave a pawn here!" Miligan shouted, exhilarated that her plan had gone off without a hitch. Indeed—during their entire conversation with Rivermoore, she'd been sending out mana frequencies into the water to lure the chimera. Handling the serpents on their own would be difficult, but by bringing in an equally dangerous creature, she could neutralize them. And once the chimera realized there were intruders in its territory, it was most likely to attack the ones giving off the most mana. Oliver was amazed at how far she'd planned ahead.

"We're in a hurry, so I'll leave this to you! Thanks, Rivermoore!"

"Charlatan...!" Rivermoore snapped, a hint of a smile playing on his lips. But even he couldn't ignore the chimera and go after them. Their boat sped up again and shot across the water, leaving the deadly battle between titans in the distance.

"Barely managed to escape that one! Someone pinch me—I must be dreaming!" Miligan exhaled a huge breath once they were out of danger.

Nanao, who had been watching behind them, then turned to her. "...Ms. Miligan, what is a Final Visitor?" she asked.

The witch had used that phrase during her conversation with Rivermoore. Miligan looked at Nanao with slight surprise. Oliver knew how she felt. Few people asked such a question at Kimberly—it was a concept nearly every student was familiar with.

"Ah, you still don't know... Well, it's something of a mage custom."

Miligan's tone was abnormally solemn. There was likely not a mage alive who wouldn't sit up a little straighter when they had to imagine the fate that would eventually befall them or their close friends.

"When a mage is consumed by the spell, another goes to care for them in their final hours—sometimes at the risk of their own life. We call that role the Final Visitor."

CHAPTER 4

The Final Hymn

When you're completely infatuated with something, you're often one of the last to realize it.

"...Which do you like more, this or this? Tell me, Carlos!"

And that was precisely the predicament Ophelia found herself in. She'd already asked Carlos the question six times, holding the same accessories up in both hands. But it was even more impressive that Carlos managed to give a unique answer each time, with nary a wrinkle of their brow.

"They're both cute, but if you asked Al, it'd be the left. He's not a fan of gaudy things."

"I—I see... Then I'll go with this one."

She took their advice and chose the left hair accessory, then excitedly put it on. Just as she finished, she realized what they'd said and rounded on them.

"...?! Wh-what was that?! No one asked about Mr. Godfrey's preferences!"

"Oh, really? Sorry, guess I jumped to conclusions."

"Isn't it obvious? Th-this is just a normal part of getting dressed...!"

Ophelia turned away haughtily, her face bright red.

Carlos smiled and shrugged as they studied her profile. "Don't get too worked up about it. Al's a simple guy at heart. A long, honest relationship is the key to getting close to him. You'd do well to remember that rushing things will only backfire."

"Like I said—!"

She turned around again to try and make more excuses, but Carlos hugged her head-on, catching her by surprise. The words died on her lips.

"Don't be so shy. You look really cute, Lia."

It was incredibly confusing. Why did her thoughts always drift to him? Why did she feel so glum when she couldn't see him?

The six months she'd spent with the neighborhood watch were full of endless confusion, following him around without a clue as to what was going on. His every word held the potential to bring her the greatest joy or sadness, and there wasn't anything more exciting in the world to her—thinking back on it, she was a total child.

"Ow-ow-ow-ow-ow-ow-ow-ow! I-I'm stuck! Someone help!"

"How many times do I have to tell you? Don't stick your hand in random places!"

And so, once again, she found herself on this day healing Tim's arm after his encounter with a cracking crab. Early on, these events gave her a huge fright, but now it was all in a day's work.

"Thanks…"

"Don't pinch your nose," Godfrey demanded. "You're being rude to her."

"It's a show of my loyalty!" Tim crowed. "I swear, my loins shall never yearn for anyone but you, Godf— Gyaaaaaaa! The painnnn!"

That said, she'd realized there was no need for mercy or compassion with someone like this. It was hardly the first time someone made a crack about her Perfume, but Tim was the only idiot to ever pinch his nose in front of her. So as an expression of respect for his bravery, she made sure once again to heal him in the most painful way possible. His high-pitched screams echoed in the dark labyrinth.

"…Sorry about that, Ophelia," said Godfrey.

"Can you be any more shameless?" Lesedi snapped. "You both pollute the air, but at least she's not so evil as to do it on purpose."

The two of them sighed as they lectured Tim, as per usual. In fact, it had become so typical because Ophelia was now a part of the group. She was among people who didn't shun her—it was such an incredibly refreshing experience for Ophelia that she felt like a new person.

"You people again... Hmm? I see you've brought an interesting morsel this time."

Of course, they ran into danger as well. Not only was it completely normal for students to carry out secret battles within the labyrinth, but Godfrey's neighborhood watch also made him a lot of enemies. Wherever they went, there was sure to be fireworks.

"Fascinating. Let's see what she can do. **Congreganta!**"

"To arms! **Flamma!**"

Godfrey blasted the charging skeletal beast with a fireball. As the flames licked up his arm after yet another failure to control the spell, he roared, "Why can't you value life more?! Not just the lives of others! Yours as well!"

On every corner of campus, in every dark cavern of the labyrinth, they fought all manner of opponents: classmates, lowerclassmen, and sometimes even monstrous upperclassmen. And through their battles, they formed a tiny measure of order within the unholy temple and tried to create a safe haven for the weak and injured. They might have been the first in Kimberly's history to try and do so.

As for why they were attempting such madness, Ophelia had no idea. Nor did she come even close to understanding Alvin Godfrey's constant rage. He was simply beyond her comprehension.

Since enrolling at Kimberly, Ophelia had never felt that something was wrong with the academy. The students dedicated their lives to the pursuit of magic, consequently trampling on everything else and killing one another. It was just like home—but most importantly, it was just like how her mother had taught her the world worked.

"...I just want to make Kimberly a place where you can relax a bit," Godfrey would sometimes say with a sigh. Ophelia always gave a noncommittal response, never really understanding. Was he talking about a place like her garden? She tried to imagine it but quickly realized that was wrong. Stomping on the flowers was all the garden was good for.

Confusingly, Godfrey apparently didn't want anyone to get trampled or downtrodden. In fact, he rejected the common notion that trampling on others was only natural. He wanted to place standardized rules on activities within the labyrinth and reduce the number of student fights—when others heard his goals, nearly all of them looked at him like he was crazy. And honestly speaking, Ophelia had felt the same at first. But shockingly enough, as he continued to spout his rhetoric in earnest, little by little, people sympathetic to his cause started appearing out of the woodwork.

"Are you guys the Godfrey Gang? Hey, hey, let me join!"

"Seems kinda fun. How about letting me in? I can give ya a hand."

As they went up in years, the students learned to adapt to Kimberly. Whether they enjoyed this, however, was another matter entirely. And those who didn't enjoy adapting were drawn to Godfrey. Not for any grand reason like sharing in his ideology—it was simply because the students who were forced to live in such a bloodthirsty environment preferred Godfrey's overall "vibe."

Some students would even confess, "I used to think I'd enrolled in the wrong school... But with you guys, it's not so bad." And for Ophelia, who couldn't understand most of her peers' feelings, this at least she could heavily sympathize with. When she was by Alvin Godfrey's side, her heart was at ease. When they interacted, she was able to forget for just a moment that she was a mage.

But even as naive as she was, Ophelia knew the hard truth—that this fantastical time could not last forever.

Every time Godfrey stuck his neck into trouble and came back in one piece, public opinion of their group rose, and little by little, their numbers swelled.

They were like campers huddled around a fire. Kimberly was a place devoid of warmth, especially the welcoming, undiscriminating kind. Any kindling was immediately extinguished.

But this fire was unprecedentedly stubborn. As people began to realize this, the stares slowly turned from bewilderment to respect. Even the upperclassmen respected Godfrey; before long, his name was known far and wide throughout the academy.

"......"

And the brighter he shone, the more the shadows near him stood out. Try as she might to stay out of the limelight, Ophelia's Perfume wouldn't allow it. Not everyone was able to overcome her aroma like Godfrey had—so, predictably, the newer members came to resent her.

"Someone should do something about her. It's just indecent."

"Stop it. You know she's Godfrey's favorite."

"You really think so? I hate to say it, but maybe he's under her spell, too."

The discord came from all directions, eating away at her heart bit by bit. The influx in members also meant that Ophelia's role of healer was not so unique anymore. This should have been a good thing; more supporters meant that Godfrey's initiatives were making real progress.

"Our little family's gotten so big so fast... It's all thanks to you, Ophelia. If you and Carlos weren't there to heal my wounds, I would've died in the labyrinth long ago, no question."

Most of all, it made her incredibly happy to hear him say those words. She wanted to hear them so much that she hated the idea of giving up her role to anyone else. It was her only way to remain by his side.

"He'll never reach his full potential with you around. You do realize that, right?"

The friction between her and the new members was endless. They came in private, pleading with her in earnest; they came in groups, threatening her. Each time, what they wanted was the same: Stay away from Godfrey.

"Your Perfume bewitches every man who comes close. That's enough to hurt the group as a whole, but worst of all is how close you are to our leader. Godfrey's greatest strength is how he will interact with anyone, regardless of who they are. But as long as you're around, people will doubt his motives."

"Everyone's thinking it. There's only one reason he'd keep such a nuisance like you around: You must've seduced him."

"...Go to hell."

It was rare for her voice to tremble with anger. She was used to being ridiculed for her Perfume, but she couldn't permit people to think that Godfrey had been seduced by it. Everything he'd put himself through just to be able to look her in the eye—the pain he'd undergone, the time he'd dedicated, the sincerity he'd shown—they were all irreplaceable treasures to Ophelia.

"Are you really going to insist that your Perfume has nothing to do with why Godfrey keeps you around? All right, then let me ask: What makes you so valuable that you deserve your spot?"

"—!"

"We know you were there in the beginning, when healers were limited. No one's trying to take that away from you. But things are different now. Plenty of us can heal just as well as you can. And unlike you, we don't cast Perfume on everyone around us."

Their argument boiled down to this: Pass the torch to someone more suitable. And they *did* have a point. Ophelia realized that her healing skills alone weren't enough to outweigh the negative of her Perfume and protect her current position.

She panicked, unable to find a way out of this argument. What should she do? What could she show these people that would prove that her place was by Godfrey's side? All she knew for sure was that she didn't have the option of giving up.

"...You think you're stronger than me?"

So she switched gears and struck back. She would help the group not by healing but by fighting. The students merely chuckled.

"Of course. Wanna test us right now, Salvadori Harlot?"

They were clearly mocking her. She'd never gotten the best grades in sword arts or spellology. She was a great healer but below average when it came to battling on the front lines. At least, that was what everyone else believed.

"...Sure. Let's do it."

The air suddenly grew heavy; the tension was palpable. The students backed away from her into spell distance, then drew their athames. Ophelia eyed them with pity. They were gravely mistaken. It wasn't because she lacked power that she avoided the battlefield—but because she didn't want Godfrey to see what she was truly capable of.

"*Partus.*"

And she wasn't wrong. What unfolded wasn't even a competition— it was a massacre.

I'm stronger than any of you. In order to protect her spot by Godfrey's side, she had to thoroughly convince others of that. The group's reaction made it clear that her position would be stolen if she stayed a meek healer. So she decided to do a complete one-eighty.

After that day, she made a point to accept every fight that came her way. Anyone who complained, she silenced with her full power; once they were weakened, she Charmed them and dominated their minds. This was what happened when she got serious.

Opponents from her own year were no big deal, but she still couldn't let down her guard against the battle-hardened second- and third-years. She dared not make an enemy of fourth-years and up. She soon needed to keep a powerful chimera in her belly at all times in order to be able to fight at a moment's notice, something she had no qualms about doing.

"Lia, stop! You don't have to do this. Al won't abandon you—"

She brushed off even her childhood friend's attempts to stop her. With her mindset changed, Ophelia danced through life like never before. She now had two purposes: desperately protect her position at Godfrey's side and weed out the members bringing their group down. Nothing held her back anymore. She would be more cunning and greedier than anyone else—just as a mage should be.

Ophelia's new stance naturally caused a chain reaction among the rest of the group. Flaunting one's own strength while defeating others in order to secure one's desired position—conflict became the new normal. The group's rapid expansion, combined with Godfrey's inability to keep an eye on every last member, became its downfall. The once peaceful vibe was lost over time, and a definitive change came over the neighborhood watch.

"That's enough! What good can come of fighting among one another?!"

Godfrey noticed this and tried to stop it, but he was too inexperienced as a leader. It would have been one thing if they had only five or six members like in the beginning, but it was nearly impossible to rein in dozens of people all at once. Day in and day out, his comrades grew more combative; unable to find a solution, he watched the stress mount.

"It's okay, Godfrey… I haven't changed at all. I'll always be by your side."

Meanwhile, Ophelia used this turmoil as an opening to cement her place by Godfrey's side. It was much more convenient for her if things stayed violent. When the group was still peaceful, someone who constantly emitted Perfume would have immediately been eliminated as a threat. There was no place for her in clear waters, but in muddied waters, a threat could lurk unnoticed.

"…Stop riling everyone up, Ophelia. I can't turn a blind eye anymore."

However, as things grew worse, people caught on to her plan. The first to speak up was another female student and founding member of the neighborhood watch: Lesedi Ingwe. She pulled Ophelia aside and gave her a warning, not an accusation.

"...What are you talking about? I haven't done anything."

"Don't play dumb. You've Charmed some of our members into being your servants. I would've overlooked it if you were just finishing fights others started, but this is clearly against the rules. If Godfrey knew, he'd never allow it."

Lesedi pierced her with a stern gaze. The emotion vanished from Ophelia's face in an instant.

"...So you agree? That a girl like me doesn't belong by Godfrey's side?"

"...? What're you babbling about? I'm talking about the group's rules—"

"You think you're a better fit for him? Is that what it is?"

Ophelia cut her off, ignoring what she had to say. Lesedi immediately grabbed her cheek in an iron grip.

"Enough crazy talk, little girl. Can you not even tell anymore when someone's on your side?"

"......"

"Listen to me. I'm warning you so that you can stay with Godfrey," Lesedi growled. "What you think you're doing, and what you're actually accomplishing, couldn't be more different. Right now, you're on a crash course for a nasty split. You need to hurry up and realize that before it's too late!"

She shoved Ophelia back, then spun on her heel. Ophelia watched her go until she was left all alone.

"...What other way is there?" she muttered.

Ophelia didn't know how to interact with other people, how to make friends, or even how to fall in love. So in all things, she acted as a mage would. Her goal was to stay by Godfrey's side, and she achieved that by any means necessary. This was the surest way to get what she wanted, after all.

"...You smell awful."

Naturally, this method meant there was a lot of collateral damage as well—including the friendships she'd taken so long to foster.

"Disgusting! I could deal with it before, but not anymore. You absolutely reek," Tim spat as they patrolled the labyrinth alone. His tone was cold, completely unlike his usual friendly ribbing. He glared at her with unbridled disdain. "Your Perfume is polluting the air at full blast... You're not even trying to control it. I bet your goal is to seduce every last male around you."

Ophelia intentionally didn't deny it. Instead, her eyes flicked to Tim's crotch. Her lips twisted in a bewitching smile.

"...You're hard, aren't you?"

"Fuck off. I don't get hard for anyone but Mr. Godfrey. I would never let you affect me."

Tim swore in disgust. Ophelia's unfettered Perfume was violating; it forced others into a state of arousal. Her oppressive Charm could even overwrite an individual's sexual orientation on occasion. So in order to resist this onslaught, Tim had to keep his mind sharp at all times.

"But you're trampling all over my feelings, crushing them into the mud. All you want is to rob me of my will and turn me into a drooling male, just like the rest of your harem...isn't that right?"

"......"

Her silence was his answer. Tim's fists shook.

"And in the end, are you going to seduce Mr. Godfrey, too? We've spent so much time together, broken bread together, risked death over and over—but that's what you really wanted all along?"

Tim's eyes wavered with rage and sadness in equal measure. Ophelia's chest twinged for a brief moment, which she immediately chalked up to a coincidence. She had no friends. She never got close enough to anyone to make her heart hurt like this in the first place. So it was all in her imagination.

"At least deny it... Tell me I'm wrong, Opheliaaaa!"

With a scream, Tim drew his athame. Ophelia's face froze into a sneer as she intercepted the attack.

The next thing she knew, the boy was lying before her like a rag. Godfrey came running over. She would never forget the anger, regret, and self-condemnation on his face.

"Godfrey, I…"

She tried to say something to the person in front of her, then realized it was just a memory from long ago. Back in reality, Ophelia was welcomed by the familiar sight of her workshop and the fledgling chimeras crawling about. Her hands shook as she looked at her wristwatch: Five hours had passed. Apparently, she had been simply sitting there daydreaming.

"…Heh-heh-heh… I can't tell the difference between a dream and reality anymore, huh? …It's finally time."

Her body was rapidly approaching its human limits. She could be consumed by the spell at any moment. With this in mind, she stood shakily from her chair.

"…I don't want it to start here… No—outside…"

She hobbled over to the door, opened it, and stepped out of the workshop. That was the beginning of her final wandering voyage as a human.

"…Her presence is fading."

Albright, who'd been listening carefully from his cell nearby, picked up on the witch's departure.

Pete swallowed, realizing what this meant.

"Now's our chance. Our first and last, probably. Are you ready?"

"…Y-yeah."

The bespectacled boy nodded without letting himself tremble. He'd made his mind up long ago—if he wanted to survive, there was no time to be afraid. Albright liked the look of determination on Pete's face.

"Let's get started. I'll lure the chimeras to me."

That was the signal—Pete took action, pouring mana into the explosive spheres they'd buried in two spots within the flesh prison. Then he quickly backed up, dropped to the floor, and covered his ears. A few seconds later, an explosive boom rattled his eardrums straight through the hands covering them. He turned around to see a hole had been ripped open in the bars.

"…!"

He tossed another sphere—which started billowing smoke—and leaped out of the prison. He had only a few precious moments until the chimeras realized what was happening and it was all over. Just as he'd practiced again and again in his mind, Pete ran toward the next room, using the smoke as cover.

"Come, wretches! I'll take on every last one of you!"

Meanwhile, Albright caught the incoming chimeras' attention. Unfortunately, he'd given his precious magical tools to Pete and was completely unarmed. If he moved too quickly, he'd inhale more of the Perfume, so he couldn't even leave the prison and run around. Pete needed to find Albright's wand quickly, or the chimeras would torture him to death.

"Wands, wands… Where are they?!"

He scanned the room and ripped open every bit of storage he could find. Ophelia could have already disposed of their things, so if he didn't find anything right away, he'd have to abandon the idea. The twenty-second time limit he'd given himself was quickly approaching.

"…There!"

Luck was on his side. Ophelia had tossed her prisoners' wands and athames into a box in the corner, apparently not even worried about the potential threat if they got back into the students' hands. First he grabbed his own, then searched for Albright's based on his descriptions.

"Here's yours! Take it!"

Pete dashed back to the prison room and tossed the athame through the bars toward Albright, who was stubbornly kicking back the fledgling chimeras. He caught it, and with a weapon now in his possession, he smiled.

"Great work! **Frigus!**"

Albright immediately cast a spell, striking back at the incoming chimeras. Pete sighed in relief, but Albright barked, "What are you doing? Get outside and call for help!"

"But you—"

"Now! Salvadori will be back once she notices something's wrong!" he shouted as he fended off the chimeras.

Pete shook off his doubts and sprinted through the door; the witch hadn't bothered to lock it. He burst out of the workshop into an unfamiliar swamp.

"Huff! Huff...!"

Escaping wasn't much of a relief. Would Ophelia come back first, or would help arrive in time? It was all up to fate now. Pete poured mana into the rescue orb, sending a shrill sound and waves of mana reverberating through the third layer.

"Please, someone help...!"

One boy in particular immediately picked up on the desperate cry.

"An SOS! He's close!" Oliver shouted as soon as he heard the orb's signal. He and the girls had already crossed the swamp, landed the boat, and begun searching the area. His eyes turned toward the source of the sound, and the other three followed suit. The chimeras could hear it, too, of course—if there was indeed a person in need of rescue there, then it was a race against time to save them.

"Not the time to be suspicious of traps. Let's move!" Miligan urged.

Oliver and the girls took off without delay. They tore through the mud, not a shred of doubt in their minds that their friend was nearby.

*　　*　　*

The third layer was so vast that the signal didn't even cover a tenth of it. However, Oliver's group weren't the only mages within its range.

"An SOS signal!"

Picking up the faint sound in the air, Carlos stopped immediately and shouted to their comrade. Godfrey cupped his hand to his ear to try and catch it but shook his head after a few seconds.

"...I can't hear it. Must be pretty far."

"I'll lead the way. Let's hurry, Al!"

Carlos began running, and Godfrey was hot on their heels. When it came to sensitivity to sounds, Carlos couldn't be beat. The two of them rushed ahead, relying on Carlos's ears to guide them.

"It's this way... Noll's friend might be there. Let's hurry, Shannon."

At the same time, Oliver's relatives-slash-vassals Gwyn and Shannon Sherwood hurried off as well. The signal was just barely audible, although Gwyn's hearing was nowhere near Carlos's. However, Oliver's cousins had no idea that he was on this layer as well.

"Lia...!" Shannon said mournfully.

Ophelia was the source of all this strife, but she wasn't just another enemy to Shannon, nor to Gwyn, either. Still, the elder Sherwood remained calm.

"Don't assume that you'll be able to reason with her. If we meet— we'll have no choice but to fight."

"...!" Shannon bit her lip at her brother's callous remark.

No matter her feelings, that fact wouldn't change. This was part of facing someone who'd been consumed by the spell.

"Mm?"

Suddenly, Gwyn stopped, as did Shannon. The clock was ticking, but they were confident in their decision.

"*Impetus!*"

Gwyn drew his athame and shot a wind spell toward the ground a few dozen yards away. The mud around the target flew into the air—revealing white bones.

"…Oh? The Sherwood siblings?"

The skeletal sphere showed itself, and within it was a man. Gwyn, who'd sensed the ambush, glared at the familiar face. "…Rivermoore?"

"It's been a while, Gwyn. I'm sure you heard the alarm, but I suggest you quit while you're ahead. If you follow it, you'll most certainly run into Salvadori. And you are not welcome near her."

The bony capsule around Rivermoore unfurled like a hand, and he stepped down onto the ground. The Sherwoods clutched their athames.

"There are too many intruders today," Rivermoore said with a shrug. "I'm only here to repel anyone other than Purgatory and Hymn, but now I have you two plus Snake Eye and her three first-year companions to deal with… Although I suppose I'm an intruder as well," he muttered with an air of self-derision. The Sherwoods couldn't believe their ears.

"Hold on. What did you just say?" Gwyn quickly asked. Rivermoore chuckled.

"Exactly what it sounded like. Snake Eye brought three first-years with her to this layer. Something about wanting to help a friend of theirs who was kidnapped."

"Who were those first-years?"

Gwyn was careful not to let his panic show.

Rivermoore put a hand to his chin and thought. "The McFarlane girl, a foolhardy samurai—and who was the other one again? …Ah, yes. Oliver Horn. We ran into each other on the first layer soon after the entrance ceremony, so I remembered his face."

The moment Oliver's name came up, Gwyn and Shannon dashed forward. They tried to catch Rivermoore by surprise and slip past him—but two skeletal serpents burst out of the mud behind him and blocked the way, as if he'd expected this.

"No, I can't let you go. Didn't you hear me? We're not welcome."

"Move, Rivermoore!" Gwyn growled, athame in hand.

Rivermoore cocked his head curiously at his reaction. "Hmm? Oddly passionate about this, aren't you? Is this Oliver of such importance?" His sneer deepened. Of course, his demeanor never changed for a moment. "Still—I must apologize. If you insist on passing, you will have to do so by force. That's the rule here, isn't it?"

Neither side was budging, so there was no sense in denying it. In perfect harmony, the Sherwood siblings jumped into battle—to carve open a path to Oliver.

"Huff! Huff! Huff...!"

Monsters crawled out of the swamp, attracted by the alarm, so Pete couldn't afford to stand still. His athame in his right hand and the rescue orb gripped tightly in his left, he ran through the marshland. His lungs burned, and his pants were muddy up to his knees.

"Where the heck am I?! Damn it, my legs...!"

With every step he took, his legs sank deeper into the mud, and he pitched forward. For Pete, who was still inexperienced in his footwork, even traversing this swamp was a herculean task. Nonetheless, he pushed forward through the mud and sludge.

"...Ugh...?!"

Suddenly, he stopped. His legs were covered to the knees and too heavy to lift. He struggled, trying to pull free, but only managed to get himself even more stuck. His face instantly blanched.

"A bottomless swamp...?! Y-you're kidding me!"

He desperately tried to calm his panicking mind; he became intensely aware of the athame in his right hand. What was the spell that would free him from this? There should have been multiple, but he couldn't think of them. Fear and frustration welled up in him. What had he spent the last six months studying for?!

"Gah...! S-someone! Someone help!"

As his mind raced, he continued sinking until his right hand was in the mud as well. He could no longer cast a spell. The chill of the mud steadily seeping into his clothes made him think of death.

"*Huff... Huff... Huff...!*"

He wanted to cry and thrash but barely managed to contain the urge. Moving would only accelerate the sinking. There was nothing he could do now, so his best option was to not move and keep breathing for a few more minutes and seconds.

"*...Blergh...!*"

The time he bought ran out in seemingly an instant, and the mud finally started pushing into his mouth. With his last moments, he took a huge breath, then was pulled mercilessly beneath the surface.

So this is where I die, he thought. Oddly enough, as despair gripped his heart, what surfaced in his mind wasn't the faces of his parents or sights from his hometown—but the face of a meddling roommate.

Oliver...!

The moment he voicelessly shouted that name, something grabbed firmly onto his wrist and pulled him, body and spirit, back to life.

"Are you okay, Pete?!"

Hearing the voice, he cautiously opened his tightly shut eyes. The last face he'd pictured was right there before him.

"*...Huh...?*"

He stared in a daze as Oliver pulled him to his feet and squeezed the mud-covered boy in a close embrace. The chill of the swamp melted away against Oliver's warmth, as if it had never existed at all.

"...You did great, Pete. You did so, so great...!"

Oliver sobbed his friend's name as he held him in his arms. Suddenly, all manner of emotions burst forth within Pete.

"Ungh... Ah—AAAAAH...!"

Oliver tossed most of his belongings onto solid ground, then lifted his crying friend onto his back and got to his feet. Nanao, Chela, and

Miligan followed close behind; they nodded to each other and the group, then picked up speed. This wasn't the time or place for joyful reunions.

"Let's hurry! If we can escape, we'll be in the clear!" Oliver shouted.

The four of them held their breath as they ran through the swamp. As hurried as they were, broomriding was out of the question. Flying on this layer would invariably draw attention from the creatures on the ground, and with Pete in tow, someone would have to ride double. If they were pursued on broomstick, this would make them easily catchable.

"Once we're past the swamp, we're home free…! Just hang in there a little longer, Pete!" Chela said to her friend as they ran.

Get in the boat and cross the swamp—this was just one way for them to escape the enemy's pursuit. It was hard to believe that Ophelia herself would come to the other side of the swamp to retrieve Pete's body. If everything went well, they could go back the way they came while avoiding being spotted by chimeras.

"Oliver…! Oliverrr…!"

Pete clung to Oliver's shoulders painfully. If they had the time, Oliver would have loved to hug him back for as long as possible. How terrifying it must have been getting abducted by that witch, and how much courage he must have needed to escape. He'd truly survived by a hairbreadth; when Oliver found him, Pete was seconds away from drowning.

"…Ah…"

They were rushing through the wetlands as quickly as possible when Miligan stopped ahead.

Oliver stopped as well, frowning. Why here? Wasn't time of the essence? He was about to ask—

"…Couldn't be that easy, I guess."

—but the moment before he could, he realized why the Snake-Eyed Witch had stopped. It was hard not to—many pairs of eyes glowed in the darkness of the marsh, completely blocking their path. He

immediately knew these creatures weren't native to this area; they had
the extreme bloodthirst of the chimeras they'd fought earlier.

"...Lots of surprising faces here. Is this a dream? Or reality...?"

A lone witch proceeded toward them, flanked by about ten familiars. One might call her a lotus in the mud, but her looks were far too
bewitching for such a comparison. Oliver's entire body shivered in
fear. Here she was, the source of this hell—Ophelia Salvadori.

"...Oh, so that's it. I was wondering how you escaped... You aren't
male, are you?" the witch said in a hushed tone toward Pete on Oliver's
back, as if a riddle had just been solved. "You switched sexes since I
captured you... A reversi? What a rare specimen my net caught..."

She sounded almost not of this world. Ophelia looked at the others—at
Nanao, Chela, then Oliver—and sighed tiredly.

"Oh, Mr. Horn. How many times must you ignore my warnings?
You should have abandoned your friend. Yet, here you are, with two
more friends in tow..."

It was hardly something she had any right to say to her victims, but
no one objected. Firmly aware of Pete's trembling, Oliver desperately
sought a way to escape despite knowing how dire the situation was.
Ophelia, unaware of any of this, looked at the last remaining person—
the one other student in her year.

"I'm impressed you all made it down here... Snake Eye, what is your
game?"

"They begged me to save their friend. And I can't deny requests from
my adorable juniors."

Perhaps as a fellow fourth-year, Miligan was able to converse with
Ophelia as if nothing was wrong. But her answer made Ophelia frown.

"I've always hated that about you. Who cares about these relation-
ships? Peel off the outer layer, and you're just like me."

"Ha-ha-ha! You're not wrong." Miligan shrugged with a self-derisive
grin, then changed the subject. "That aside, I have something to ask—
can you let us go? Our only business down here is to rescue Pete. I'd

hate to disturb you at such a pivotal moment of your life, so why don't you let us go and forget we were ever here?"

"……"

"Losing Pete isn't going to affect your efforts, right? We have no reason to interfere, and you have more important things to do than squabble with us. It's a total win-win, don't you think?"

Miligan's tone was upbeat, but Oliver listened with bated breath. Their only remaining hope was for Ophelia to let them go. Now that they were face-to-face, their fates were almost entirely in her hands. The one thing they needed to avoid was getting involved in a fight.

"Let's part ways amiably, okay? Oh, but you deserve something to make up for Pete's loss. I can give you a rare magic potion. What do you say?"

Miligan was clearly trying to steer things in this direction as well. Oliver had no idea her chances of success. All he knew was that he didn't feel the slightest twinge of optimism.

"…How absurd, Snake Eye. You think you're still talking to a human?"

Ophelia grinned pityingly, as if to prove Oliver's hunch right. Now he and Chela knew for sure—this conversation had been pointless all along.

"Don't misunderstand me. I didn't come here to specifically bring back an escapee," Ophelia explained. "I could sense people, so I was just idly strolling toward them. I was in search of a place to *begin*; that place just happened to be here…"

No one could stop her, just as humankind cannot prevent the sun from sinking below the horizon.

Bestia alas petito, avis manus invidus, piscis pedes cupiditas, planta carnem desiderat.

The beast desires wings, the bird envies hands, the fish seeks legs, the tree idolizes flesh.

*   *   *

And so it began. Like a cup overflowing with wine, the words spilled from her mouth.

"Stop that chant!" Miligan yelled, all composure now vanished from her face. Nanao and Chela immediately drew their athames, and Oliver did as well once he set Pete down. The chimeras behind Ophelia moved in front to protect their master.

Quamquam decem milia fient semina, quae sata sunt sed tamen nemo, nostrum vitium non habet.
The scattered seeds reach far, yet we all have a piece.

At this point, there was no time to analyze each chimera for a weakness to exploit. Chela shifted to her elven form and fired off a double incantation at the wall of monsters, trying to pierce a hole. She burned the head of one, but the resulting gap was filled by another in mere seconds. Nanao and Oliver, who had charged toward the gap, were forced to skid to a halt.

Congregans fragmenta et continuans de incubus haec volebam scire, ubi solutio vitae est?
Gather the pieces, patch them together. Wherein lies the answer to life?

Miligan followed up with a spell of her own. Spears of fire and ice made a beeline straight for Ophelia. The chimeras' tentacles extended and blocked the attack, rebuffing Nanao and Oliver, who were rushing in on broomsticks. The creatures' antiair abilities were rock-solid and prevented any half-baked aerial strikes.

Quaestio infinita quamvis per multos annos haec investigatio de anima facta esset non dum exitum in veniat.
Even if the question is answered and eternity is overcome, life's searchings will never abate.

*   *   *

Mana coursed through Miligan's entire body. Unleashing the reserve mana in her womb and amplifying her output, she cast another spell. Not a double-incantation but a *triple*-incantation fire spell—she bet victory on the raw power of a spell that was impossible for anyone but a seasoned mage. Oliver and his friends watched as three chimeras were swallowed by waves of flames in an instant.

Si tacito bene est. Respondebo igitur a deam qua excitam per hunc rituum infinitum.
But no matter. Find the solution within the endless formula.

They knew this was their last chance, and they took off. Hiding among the flames, they slipped through the wall of chimeras. The moment the three of them were through, a new chimera dropped from the ceiling to block the way. Its body was covered in bedrock and was unlike anything they'd seen before.

Liquamini miscenimi que inter sese animi hic vobis licet temptare et errare in perpetuum.
Intermingling lives, I permit you infinite experimentation here and now.

The four of them stopped. If there was even the tiniest opening available, they were all prepared to take it no matter the cost. Unfortunately, there was nothing. They couldn't imagine a single way to break through. The only thing Oliver could do was retreat toward Miligan with Nanao and Chela so as to avoid being trapped by the chimeras.

Delectemini luxuriate ad sempiternum quoniam hic ritus spiritus generat.
Bask in the unending debauchery if therein lies life's formula.

＊　　＊　　＊

Ophelia's chant continued unabated, echoing loud and clear. Oliver racked his brain for a way out; without a plan, he could only make guesses. The same was true for Nanao, Chela, and even Miligan.

Ludite in mea placenta amabili fetus quotiens moriemini totiens ego ipsa concipiam.
Beloved children dancing in my womb, if we must die, then we must give birth many times over.

A terrible ringing assaulted their ears. All sights and sounds warped; the laws that held this world together crumbled until there was nothing left. Pete, afraid of witnessing this with his own eyes, grabbed his head and cowered on the ground. He doubted his sanity would survive otherwise.

Utinam tu clamoribus nativitates iugiter impleariso—Palatium animalum!
Fill the air with endless screams of birth—Palatium animalum!

This was the basis upon which the chant was constructed. Everything vanished and was replaced.

All of a sudden, the four of them were looking at a sky covered in pulsating flesh. Numerous veins of varying sizes ran along the ground, which contracted and dilated with the flow of blood. They could feel the unmistakable warmth of a living being.

"...!"

The sight was at once vomit-inducing and strangely familiar. They seemed to instinctually know where they were. Perhaps their minds didn't remember it, but their bodies did—it was the place where life began.

They were in utero, encased within a massive womb constructed of mana.

"...Oliver, what is all this?" asked Nanao.

"It's...an aria." Oliver struggled to answer. The heavy scent of Perfume flowed through his nostrils and into his brain. He felt like he was going to lose his mind by just breathing. He quickly bit his cheek, using the pain to keep himself grounded while Chela picked up where he left off.

"...A Grand Aria. The final destination for a mage who has mastered their craft," she began. "Unlike spells that simply activate magical phenomena within the real world, the mana unleashed from a Grand Aria completely rewrites reality. Like painting something new atop an old painting..."

Chela's voice was filled with fear, awe, and a kernel of respect. Being consumed by the spell wasn't all that uncommon, but reaching that state through a Grand Aria was exceedingly rare. Only the most special individuals—perhaps the descendants of the oldest families or individuals who overcame reason in seclusion—were granted such a privilege. No one would object to calling this a mage's ultimate form.

"That's right. At the tender age of eighteen, she's finally accomplished the Salvadori line's magical pursuits. She is, without a doubt, a genius." Miligan quickly extinguished the envy that had seeped into her voice and sharply eyed their surroundings. At first glance, there appeared to be no exit from the world that had engulfed the four of them. If this was truly a womb made of magic, then it stood to reason that a birth canal connecting them to the outside world should exist. But placing hope on this wasn't just optimistic—it was delusional.

"We've been ripped from the real world and placed in another—and the one who created it sets the rules. We can't get out on our own, and no one will come from the outside to save us. Either the caster undoes the spell or we die here," Miligan continued, as if to impress on them that this really was their one and only "hope."

"That's..."

Several protuberances grew from the fleshy ground as Oliver and the girls tried to comprehend what had happened. They swelled like giant tumors before splitting open, as otherworldly creatures crawled from them, screeching like newborns. Each baby chimera was unique in its composition.

"'...Find the solution within the endless formula...'"

Oliver muttered the phrase still ringing in his ears. Now he was starting to vaguely understand what it meant.

A chimera was an experiment in creating the "perfect specimen." Every living being on this planet has some kind of deficiency; however, some believed that among the finite combinations of all living beings there lay a "correct answer." Those individuals sought a combination that didn't exist in nature.

The Salvadori progenitors—pure-blooded succubi—were said to be one such group, seeking the correct answer through male seed. Unfortunately, they had been wiped out before they were able to achieve their goal. Because they'd focused so heavily on a single correct answer, they ended up going extinct when they couldn't find it.

"...!"

Oliver forced the gears in his mind to turn in order to resist the effects of the encroaching Perfume and maintain his ability to reason.

Didn't the Salvadoris object to the very idea of a perfect life-form as a result of their failures? They considered change and evolution and the process of eternal trial and error to be the essence of life. That's what led them to decide that the unlimited diversity produced from these methods was the key to longevity...

"Wh-what the heck?! Oh my God, this can't be happening...!"

A panicked voice interrupted his train of thought, and Oliver instinctively turned toward the source. Twenty yards away from their group were two female students—one looking about frantically and another younger one in tow. The moment she spotted them, Chela looked as if someone had punched her.

"Stacy?! What are you doing here?"

"...Collateral damage, huh? Bad luck," said Miligan.

Oliver figured she must be right. These two had probably heard the emergency signal and come running, staying far enough away to not get involved with Ophelia, yet were taken by surprise by her Grand Aria. Unfortunately for them, it was literally nothing more than a stroke of rotten luck.

"I hate to say this, but we don't have many options... You three know what we need to do?" Miligan asked Oliver and the girls, and they silently drew their athames. They'd promised their friends back on campus that they'd all come back safely. So...

"...Good answer. Mages aren't allowed the privilege of despair!"

The Snake-Eyed Witch's lips curled into a sneer—the very picture of her indomitable will. That roused Nanao for battle, too, dyeing her hair a brilliantly pure white with mana. So began their final resistance.

"Fortis flamma!"

A surge of intense flames signaled the start of the battle. Miligan initiated with massive firepower, keeping at bay the chimeras that had been born prior to Ophelia's Grand Aria. Against these numbers, it was imperative that they scatter the enemy's forces. With utter calm, she started from there.

"Lynette, put up a barrier! Someone needs to be in charge of defense! You've always been decent at spatial magic, haven't you?!"

"Here?! It would barely last a few moments!"

Suddenly called to assist, Stacy's sister, Lynette Cornwallis, fell to the ground and began drawing a magic circle, practically beside herself. Oliver, frankly, was nothing but grateful. A barrier maintained by a fourth-year should be able to withstand the chimeras for at least a little bit. It would give their group temporary refuge and allow them to survive a few minutes longer than anywhere else.

"O-Oliver...!"

"Wait here, Pete! I swear we'll figure this out!"

Once Pete had evacuated to the still-forming magic circle, Oliver turned his attention to the incoming chimeras. Which one should he fight first? *How* should he fight them? No matter how much he strategized, he still came up lacking. Just one required life-risking tactics to take down, and now his entire vision was filled with them.

"Where's Fay?! Give me back Fayyyy!"

"Calm down, Stacy! Let's do this together!"

Chela stood next to her childhood friend, who was about to break from their ranks at any moment, and began chanting a spell in her elf form. Repelling the chimeras hinged on her and Miligan, their strongest casters. Oliver's and Nanao's jobs were to keep the chimeras away from them at all costs.

"Haaaaaah!"

"Ohhhhhh!"

And so they began their seemingly endless battle, fighting back the infinite oncoming waves.

Tentacles lashed out tirelessly; scythes swung; poisonous fluids belched. Nanao sidestepped, parried, and dodged every last attack, her blade often finding purchase in enemy flesh. Meanwhile, Oliver's spells razed their enemies, blinding them with light, shooting scorching flames, and summoning decoys to distract with noise.

The techniques they'd learned from Miligan were on full display here. If they didn't use them, they wouldn't have lasted more than a second. A single mistake—a single decision delayed by a second—would lead to instant death. If one of them fell, the whole group would crumble. They had to fight with literally everything they had or there would be no surviving this place.

"...How wonderful... I didn't know you could...fight so well...," came a voice.

From within the mass of endlessly spawning chimeras rose a beautiful yet repulsive woman. From below the waist, she was no longer human; it was more accurate to say she was a torso grown from the fleshy floor. It was Ophelia Salvadori, master of this world—or perhaps the world itself.

"I'm surprised your personality's still intact! So how's it feel to be consumed by the spell, Salvadori?" Miligan shouted as soon as she noticed her.

Ophelia looked down at her completely morphed form, opening and closing her hands repeatedly as if to test it out. She smiled.

"…It's…the worst… Just as I thought. But…I think I can last a little longer…until I see you all dead…!"

"Ha-ha! Thanks for the hospitality!" Miligan replied, then roasted one of Nanao's chimeric foes with a double incantation. It really wasn't the time to be joking around, yet Miligan focused her gaze on the transformed witch and teased, "Don't you know when to lie down and die?! I'm guessing you've got some big regrets!"

She unleashed the pointed comment like a flung dagger. Ophelia's shoulders momentarily twitched.

"…What…did you say?"

"I'm right, aren't I? Otherwise you'd never dig your heels in so deep. Is there some hole in you left unfulfilled after four years at the academy? Ha-ha-ha—I can hardly blame you! Your first love was quite a tragedy, after all!" Miligan cackled dramatically.

Ophelia's fists shook at the obvious bait. "Shut…up…"

"Oh, was I right? Sorry about that. Still—youth is no excuse for ignorance. President Godfrey was always out of your league. It's like a swamp snake falling in love with a unicorn: It could never work out. Even a child could tell you that."

It was at this moment that Oliver realized what Miligan was doing—she was fanning the disturbance in Ophelia's mind. If she still had her human personality, it could be their ticket to cracking her armor. That is, if this fearsome overlord of their new reality still had a heart capable of wavering.

"The best you could've hoped for was to seduce him with your Perfume and steal his seed. Ignore people's feelings and prioritize results—isn't that how your family does things? That's what happens when you're descended from succubi. I'm impressed—I could never pull that off. As a fellow mage, I wouldn't *debase* myself like that!"

"SHUT UUUUUUUUUUPPP!"

Her probing had finally hit the mark. The chimeras changed tactics from targeting everyone equally to converging on Miligan with every intent to kill her. It was as if they shared in their mother's raw fury.

""*Magnus fragor!*""

But this was Miligan's goal. The moment all the chimeras' sensory organs were focused on her, Miligan and Chela cast a spell at maximum capacity—completely covering the area in light and explosive noise.

"Ugh...?!"

To Ophelia and the chimeras, this was akin to getting dirt thrown directly in their eyes. For a moment, they were unable to sense a thing from the ensuing blinding flash. It lasted only a few seconds—but that was enough for the Snake-Eyed Witch to act.

Miligan jumped onto her broom mid-cast, using the scant reprieve from tentacle attacks to fly over Ophelia's head and immediately hop off her broom.

"...!"

Ophelia recovered her vision just before Miligan landed and instantly lashed out at the enemy figure rushing toward her. Tentacles extended from her lower half, quickly restraining Miligan's hands and feet.

"Guh!"

She was barely a step away from piercing Ophelia with her blade. They were close enough to see into each other's eyes. From behind Miligan's frazzled bangs flashed the light of her basilisk eye—and in its dark gaze, Ophelia was completely immobilized.

"That really got to you, huh? Even now, you're as human as they come, Salvadori!"

Still glaring at her opponent, Miligan quickly shed her robe and freed herself from the tentacles. Her legs were caught, but with wand and mouth still available, she could cast a spell. There could be no missing at this distance. She prepared to utter the spell that would end it all when—

"Gah—!"

—a new tentacle thrust out from her chest. It had pierced her from the back and skewered her lungs.

"…Fool. I overcame the basilisk's curse long ago," Ophelia spat.

"Ms. Miligan!" Oliver shouted, realizing their plan had failed. Ophelia didn't even spare him a glance, continuing to study the prey caught in her tentacles.

"Say those words again. What about me?"

The tentacle around Miligan's arm tightened until it broke bone, and she dropped her sword to the ground. With a punctured lung, there was no hope of fighting back—but she refused to keep her mouth shut. She refused to stop laughing at her opponent.

"…Didn't…hear me the first…time?" Miligan asked. "I said you still can't let go. Even when you've reached the peak of magehood, you still cling to the regrets of a sweet young girl. This, from a Salvadori! A family known for reveling in lewdness and carnal desire! …Ha-ha-ha-ha-ha! I can't think of anything more hilarious—!"

Two more tentacles drilled into Miligan's abdomen. Ophelia made no attempt to cover her opponent's mouth—it would only stifle the screams she wished to hear. She gazed upon her prey writhing in pain.

"…So you wish to die the worst possible death?" she said coldly. "I'll give you the gift of choice: What would you like impaled next?"

"Kah—ahhhh!"

Miligan flailed as her innards were violated with agonizing pain. Ophelia watched her victim up close, yet her gaze was hardly filled with sadism. Her expression was twisted as she gnashed her teeth. "I don't…I don't—I don't have any regrets!!"

In escaping the light, her feet naturally brought her to the deep dark of the labyrinth. The second layer was still too bright for her tastes. The third layer, however, was wonderful. Everything was dank and grimy as far as the eye could see, and best of all, hardly anyone came this way. Everyone either avoided this section or tried to move through it as quickly as possible. It was the perfect place to start her lair.

"...Lia."

Yet, there was one oddball who pursued her anyway. At their young age, it was incredibly dangerous to go this deep into the labyrinth alone—but they came just the same. Of course, they knew she didn't want to see anyone—no matter who it was.

"...Go away, Carlos. This is my territory."

Her back still turned to her childhood friend, she rejected them coldly. There was no other way. She didn't want them to risk the danger, nor did she want to be seen in her current state. Carlos Whitrow, however, had other ideas.

"Let's go back to the academy. I'll smooth things over with everyone."

"Don't be stupid."

She could never agree to that. How was she supposed to face everyone now? Not only had she spread her Perfume throughout the group and thrown it into chaos, but she'd also nearly killed one of its members and fled. She'd destroyed any sense of trust and friendship they'd developed for her.

"Don't despair. If we talk it out, Al will forgive you. You should know that—"

She knew they'd say that...and they were most likely correct. Alvin Godfrey would never abandon someone as long as they were sincere with him. No matter how many times it took—he would forgive over and over.

"......"

Which was why she couldn't face him. Her heart hurt every time he forgave her—broke, even. No matter how much she pined for his light, there was no changing the succubus blood flowing through her veins.

The more she grew to care for him, the more time they spent

together, the more she longed to steal him away entirely. She'd often catch herself having the sweetest nightmare in the corner of her mind, of unleashing her Perfume in its entirety and putting him under her spell. And every time, it made her despair.

So in order to escape that suffering—in order to reject his kindness—she gave herself no other out so that she would never return. She would never even think of poking her head into the sun again.

"…?!"

When Ophelia turned around, everything fell into place for Carlos. Her belly was swollen—and inside it was a non-chimera life.

"Lia. You…"

"…An older student asked, and I let him impregnate me. Nothing big. This is my role in life, isn't it?" Ophelia said dryly as her childhood friend struggled to find words.

This was another of the duties of those born to the Salvadori name: share the family blood among long-standing clans who showed interest. It was hardly a rare occurrence in the magical world, and Ophelia had no real reason to shirk her duty. Her body was accustomed to giving birth; she'd done it dozens of times before. One more wouldn't even make her flinch—or so the older student must have thought when he planted his seed within her.

"……"

No, she wouldn't flinch. The only thing that cried out was her heart. Lately, however, she'd started growing numb to it. She'd long accepted that she was a convenient vessel and that her heart was no more than an accessory to its function.

Yet, why was her childhood friend so visibly distraught? She'd told them nothing could hurt her anymore. Why did they suffer in her stead?

"…I told you to wait at least three years—"

"I know what you said. And I don't have any reason to listen to you," she replied icily. This was her duty as a mage. A mere guardian had no right to complain about the business of the house of Salvadori.

"I'll say this one last time: begone, Carlos. Or are you going to try and kill me, here and now?" Ophelia asked, placing a hand on her athame. If Carlos truly insisted on having their way and staying true to their path, they'd have to fight her like any other mage. Their only choice was to crush the girl before them and all the Salvadori history that came with her.

"......!"

Of course, she knew they couldn't choose that.

"...I'll be back. And I'll keep coming back until you listen," Carlos vowed, then reluctantly turned on their heel. They'd probably come again many times. And every time, she'd chase them away. She'd freeze her heart and reject any and all kindness extended to her.

"Hmph. Fallen this far, have you, succubus? How laughably predictable."

The depths of the labyrinth were filled with a surprising number of similar stories. One particular mage who gathered the bones of the dead to use as his familiars belittled her with unique turns of phrase, smiled with pity, and welcomed her to her new home:

"Rejoice, for the waters here are perfect for you. It is a most suitable location—far more palatable than the surface."

Ophelia couldn't agree more. It was such a relief to be surrounded by those like her. Now, she was free to return their loathing.

"Partus."

She responded with a spell.

Cyrus Rivermoore's mocking smile deepened. "Ha! That's the first thing you have to say to me? Seems you've built up quite a bit of resentment. Very well—this, too, is my duty as your predecessor. Let's play, shall we?"

The man chanted a spell of his own, encouraged by her hostility. Deadly duels were good for relieving stress, and she would never be without a partner again.

*   *   *

"...I realize I might be meddling, but I think you should stop."

Every now and again, she ran into Kevin Walker, too. He was one of the few older students on good terms with Godfrey's group, having personally saved them countless times.

"People may plumb the labyrinth's depths, but it's no place to make a home. Take it from me, someone who comes down here regularly: I make sure to never forget that line. Then again, this is Kimberly—as lawless a place as you'll find. But at the end of the day, it's a place for humans. There are good folks and bad, nice parts and awful parts... Kimberly's all of that. It's a place where we can laugh and cry in equal measure."

Ophelia couldn't decide how to deal with him. He was clearly different from the others who made their domains down here, yet he'd also "survived" in the labyrinth the longest of anyone. If she tried to grab him, he'd easily slip through her fingers—truly an all-around annoying person.

"Carlos is still trying their best to create a place for you. They're forming a group of students with sex-based idiosyncrasies so that you won't stand out. Are you really okay with letting things go on this way?"

He never poked his nose in for too long, typically making a few comments before leaving. But those few comments always managed to sting. Truly, he was maddening.

"...It hurts...doesn't it?"

But the most troubling person was this girl. They'd interacted a few times while Ophelia was still on the surface, but ever since she'd started living in the labyrinth, the girl would try to talk to her whenever they met.

"...How about...some tea?" she asked haltingly. "I...um, have some nice leaves... I'm good at it... Making tea, I mean."

And then she had the gall to extend such an invitation with a smile. Ophelia had no idea what to do with this puppy that had imprinted on her. If it was just a cursory bit of pity, she'd have no problem shooing her away—but she realized that this girl, at least, felt nothing of the sort.

"…Tea? Here? Don't make me laugh."

It pained Ophelia to coldly scoff at her every time they met. Usually, the girl was accompanied by her older brother. He was also a friend of Carlos's, which made him doubly annoying.

"If you don't like it down here, then let's go up," the boy said. "Not to the surface, no. But the second layer would be better, wouldn't it?"

"Why don't you try grabbing me by the collar and dragging me, Sherwood?"

When Ophelia rejected them, the girl always looked so sad. Ophelia hated seeing that—so this was the one person she turned her back on first.

"If that's all, then you can leave. I'll pass on licking each other's wounds."

This was the truth, really. Spending her time with someone who bore the same pain was no better than staring at a broken mirror.

"…You're going to give back my comrades, Ophelia."

It was inevitable that this incident came to pass after she'd chosen the life of a labyrinth witch. She abducted people when her research required it, sapped them of their vitality, and tinkered with their minds and bodies with utter impunity. So naturally, she ended up clashing with *him*.

"Did you come all this way just to see me, Godfrey? How perfect. These ones just ran out of juice."

Because she knew this meeting was inevitable, she'd done all she could to prepare for it. It was no coincidence that she'd abducted

Godfrey's comrades. She made him watch as her chimeras carried the students' lifeless bodies and dumped them unceremoniously onto the muddy ground.

"...Ah... A-ah..."

"You're okay now! I'm right here! Stay with me...!" Godfrey cradled each student in turn, calling out to them. Their vacant pupils barely managed to focus on him.

"Ah—gyah—gaaaaaaaaaah!!"

"...?!"

Suddenly, screams burst from their lips. Three of the students arched their backs in excruciating pain. Godfrey watched in horror as alien arms burst from their abdomens, tearing through skin and muscle.

"Wha—?!"

Three chimeras crawled out of their stomachs, wriggling in the pools of blood spilled from the hosts they'd devoured.

Godfrey was still as a stone; Ophelia gave him a radiant smile.

"Such healthy babies, aren't they? I think boys should experience the miracle of birth as well. Anyway, you're free to take them home now. These three went quite mad from the process, unfortunately. But wouldn't it be lovely if they could regain their sanity?"

She delivered each word of her prepared speech with careful accuracy. Godfrey's allies, who had been standing behind him, jumped out upon witnessing the horror. They burned the chimeras crawling at their feet with magic, then proceeded to try and save their screeching friends.

"...Your heart has been stained by the labyrinth's darkness, too."

The scene cleared Godfrey's mind of all remaining doubt. He could forgive a mistake any number of times. But there was no forgiveness in his heart for those who hurt and belittled his allies with clear malicious intent.

Godfrey drew the athame from his waist and pointed its tip at Ophelia. With unwavering spirit, he prepared to battle the enemy before him.

"No more words. This ends now. Draw, Salvadori!"

For the first time since they'd met, he called her by her family name.

"Of course."

The word was like a blade in her heart, and she raised her athame. An odd sense of peace spread throughout Ophelia's body.

She didn't need to suffer anymore. She didn't have to struggle pathetically in the light. *This* was her true form. She had finally become an enemy of humanity.

"......No...regrets......"

Ophelia's voice was shaky and weak. Her body defied human reason, yet her human memories still tortured her. And as a result of this internal discord, the chimeras were very clearly slowing down. Their relentless pressure was letting up.

Oliver hopped back and called out to his friends.

"The chimeras are losing their edge—their mother's confused! This is our last chance. Can everyone move?"

"Yes!"

"Indeed, I can."

Chela and Nanao immediately agreed. They must have been at the very limits of their stamina and mana, but they refused to show weakness.

"I can fight, too...!"

"It's all I can manage to keep this barrier up! Anything else is up to the rest of you, got it?!"

"...!"

The Cornwallis sisters indicated that they were ready as well. Pete, meanwhile, did his best to keep his hands from trembling as he gripped his athame. Oliver couldn't be more grateful. None of them had despaired, against all odds.

Upon returning his gaze to the front, he could see Miligan was still in the grasp of Ophelia's tentacles. He couldn't tell if she was conscious, but it was clear as day that she'd risked her life to create an opening for them.

"We'll act as decoys. It's up to you, Nanao," Oliver said, broom in hand, and Chela quickly picked up what he was implying. Normally, he would never choose such a method. It was a huge gamble, but at this point, there was no other choice but to ignore the risks. "We'll draw the chimeras' attacks," he continued. "While we're doing that, you fly in as fast as you can toward Ophelia Salvadori and chop off her head. That'll end it."

Oliver was frustrated with himself. This was hardly anything as grand as a "strategy"—it was simply a four-person suicide mission. He wasn't even shouldering most of the burden. It all depended on Nanao's broomriding abilities.

"I see—understood."

But Nanao didn't balk. If Oliver proposed the plan, then she'd believe in it as if it were foolproof. And that honest bravery was reason enough for Oliver to bet it all on her.

"Then that's it. Let's move!"

As the one who had suggested the plan, Oliver made sure he was the first decoy in the air. Chela and Stacy quickly mounted their brooms and flew after him. The chimeras were disorganized due to Ophelia's confusion, and they reacted instinctively to the movement. The ones with antiair capabilities focused their efforts skyward.

"We've got their attention! Now, Nanao!"

"Haaaaah!"

While the tentacles on the ground reached up for the three of them, Nanao hopped on her broom last and took off. She gained altitude in an arc, then rocketed down straight toward Ophelia.

"Uwah!"

"Stacy!"

Infinite tentacles assailed the three decoys. After a few seconds, one made contact with Stacy's broom. She lost her balance in midair, and Chela watched as she helplessly plummeted to the ground.

"Not yet! Not yet…!" Oliver muttered as he weaved between incoming tentacles. He couldn't fall yet. Not until Nanao delivered the final blow!

"Guh?!"

The ferocity of the attack took him off guard. The moment he thought he'd evaded the three tentacles, a sticky thread flew in from behind and latched onto the broom's handle. As he struggled to maintain his balance, he noticed out of the corner of his eye a spider-based chimera spitting thread. It was faster and harder to see than the tentacles, so it would be difficult to avoid no matter how much focus he gave it.

"Gah…!"

He fell a few seconds after Stacy, separating from his broom, and tumbled across the fleshy ground. Fortunately, he managed to soften his fall. The moment he recovered, he witnessed the last decoy, Chela, get tangled in the spider's thread and knocked out of the sky.

His eyes flitted to their last hope.

"Haaaaah!"

A deluge of tentacles that Oliver's group had failed to keep busy now raced toward Nanao as she made a beeline for Ophelia. With incredible maneuvering, she managed to avoid them, but the second attack wasn't so kind: A web of spider's thread stretched in front of her path, creating an impassable, unbending wall.

"*Flamma!*"

But the next moment, Nanao's fire spell pierced a hole in that wall. She'd trained hard under Oliver's tutelage so that she would have more than her sword skills available in a battle—and here, in the most critical of moments, her training bore fruit.

"Have at thee!"

Once she was through the web, there was nothing standing between Ophelia and her. Oliver watched, forgetting to breathe, as Nanao rode the momentum of her broom, her blade closing in on her enemy's neck.

*   *   *

That was when she made a fatal mistake: She locked eyes with the witch who was bawling like a little girl.

"—!"

Her sword came to a screeching halt mid-swing. The blow that should have signaled the end to the battle slipped past the witch's neck by a fraction, cutting nothing but air.

"Nanao!"

The Azian girl crashed into the ground, completely unprepared for her landing. Oliver happened to have fallen near the crash site, and he ran over, his face pale. He found Nanao lying there.

"...Forgive me, Oliver..."

Unable to get up, she still managed to offer a firm apology. Oliver approached her, hardly thinking. He didn't need to be a doctor to see that she was injured all over. Her arms, legs, and ribs were broken, along with numerous other bones. It was a miracle she was even conscious.

"...!"

He knelt next to her and cast a healing spell. He could sense the chimeras closing in around them but chased it out of his mind. He had neither the mana nor the strength to mount any sort of resistance. More importantly, he had to tend to the girl in front of him.

"...Why...didn't you kill her...? That was our last chance...," Oliver said as he healed Nanao. That should have been the end. Nanao's strike would have perfectly severed Ophelia's head. If she hadn't hesitated, everything would be over now.

"...That was...a child," came Nanao's faltering reply, recalling the moment. She'd been prepared to face a fearsome enemy, to instantly slay a demon that held no regard for human hearts and minds. That was how her battle with Ophelia Salvadori was supposed to play out. She had never expected something so childishly frail and fleeting, so infantile—the tear-stained face of a defenseless little girl.

"...I cannot kill a crying child. I just cannot."

"...!"

Oliver clenched his jaw tightly. He understood everything. With no reply to offer her, he silently leaned in to her. It was an incredibly Nanao-like reason to spare the enemy.

The end was coming. Chela was still capable of some movement and dragged her aching body over to Stacy, who'd crashed first. Picking up the immobile girl in her arms, she somehow managed to get her into the barrier where Pete and Lynette stood. This would be where she made her last stand—she resolutely drew her athame.

"...I'm sorry, Pete," she said.

"Huh...?"

"I wish I could've protected you to the very end."

The moment he heard her apology, something inside Pete burst.

"Wha—? Wait, what're you—?" Lynette stammered.

He ignored Lynette's attempts to stop him, then strode up to a shocked Chela and drew his athame.

"Don't..."

He knew it hardly made a difference. But he had to do it anyway.

"Don't apologize. You all came to save me, didn't you...?!"

The witch's heart was pure chaos inside.

Her thoughts and emotions in disarray, she could only writhe in pain and loneliness. Why she was so sad, she didn't know. There shouldn't have been any reason to be.

She'd gotten this far by doing what she was meant to. As the product of a thousand years of history—as the end to a thousand-year search— she'd completed the Salvadoris' magical pursuit in the greatest form possible. What could she possibly be unhappy about after such an amazing achievement?

"Ah... Ahhh..."

In the center of the encroaching circle of chimeras was that boy, risking his life by holding a girl who was injured from head to toe in an effort to protect her. As she watched the scene play out, Ophelia wondered when was the last time she'd been held.

"Watch this. I'll teach you how to handle males."

Her mother was teaching her secrets, body intertwined with a man she'd Charmed into mindless servitude.

"Hee-hee-hee… See? Easy, isn't it? Bait him with the pleasures of the flesh, and he'll end up just like this."

As she moved her hips, only meaningless moans escaped the man's lips. In exchange for the one-sided pleasure, his vitality was forcefully taken from him. Ophelia recalled feeling, even at a young age, that it seemed terribly pathetic.

"This isn't sex, and it certainly isn't lovemaking. This is *feeding*. We are predators, and these are our prey. The intercourse might get a little involved, but it's never anything more than a means of procuring their exceptional stock."

She'd accepted her mother's claims without any doubts. But in hindsight, they were only half-true.

"…Mother…where's Father?"

Once, when she was about fourteen years old, she wandered the house on wobbly legs two days after a difficult chimera birth that had taken a whole three days, only to realize she couldn't find her father anywhere. When she asked her mother, who was practically drowning herself in alcohol in the living room, the answer was immediate:

"I threw him out. He expelled his seed, so I had no more use for him."

Ophelia felt neither shock nor sadness, only quiet acceptance. *Ah, I figured as much.* She'd long since picked up on her father's desire to leave them. She'd always expected this day to come.

"He looked so incredibly relieved to get out of here," Ophelia's mother continued. "He had some promise, but in the end, he was just a male. He could never keep up with the Salvadori pursuits."

Except for their seed, males were entirely unnecessary to the Salvadoris' sorcery. That much was a given, considering the uterus was the key to their craft. However, Ophelia wondered, why had he stayed so long, then? Why had her mother kept her father around?

"...Why do you look so upset? Don't tell me you miss him."

Noticing her daughter's dubious gaze, the mother glared at her. She was playing dumb; Ophelia might as well have been talking to a mirror.

"Don't worry. I may be rid of him, but I have plenty of other males. Oh! With that nasty business out of the way, I should go on a hunt. It's been far too long."

And so she ran from reality. She ignored the feelings that lay dormant in her heart in order to avert her eyes from the truth—in order to maintain her family's pride as plunderers who disposed of men once they were through with them.

"Yes, let's do that. Ophelia, you're coming with me. You can have a laugh at the pitiful males as they fail to resist their own lust! That'll brighten your mood! Yes, I'm sure of it!"

The hint of madness in her mother's tone told Ophelia the truth: *Oh—we were the ones thrown away.*

"...Ah...ah......"

She'd known all along. Male, female—it made no difference so long as there was kindling for the fires that drove sorcerous pursuits. There had never been a single human in that house.

Why, then, did they continue to play out this crude performance? Why did her mother marry like a human, run a household like a human, give birth to a child like a human? Why did she give her daughter a human name like Ophelia?

"…Ahh…ahhhhhh…!"

She should never have had a name. Even a mind capable of thought was too much. If she was born to be nothing more than a womb, then there was no reason for her body to burn with such pain. She would never have had to experience the fear of love or taste the bitterness of heartbreak. The end would have come before she was forced to come to terms with any of it. Or with the fact that she was all alone.

Where is that lonesome girl?

"…?"

Her heart was about to burst screaming in an endless hell and clawing at her chest, and yet she clung to it—and then suddenly, she heard a familiar song.

Where is that little crybaby?

At first, she thought it was welling up from deep within her memories. But no—it wasn't coming from her head. It was ringing in her ears.

Don't hide. Come to me. Your tears won't dry on their own.

The gentle voice melted everything away, loosening the tight bonds this world was made of.

"Huh…?"

Oliver was the first to notice the change. A pure light shone through a space near him before slowly expanding. A bridge between their closed world and the outside was forming.

"Made it…"

Across the bridge came two figures: One, tall and muscular, was Alvin Godfrey. The other was also familiar to Oliver and his friends—a slender, androgynous youth.

"Carlos…?!"

Ophelia recognized her childhood friend and called their name in a daze. Carlos looked straight back at her and smiled softly.

"Sorry I'm late," they said. "I've come for you, Lia."

"…! Stay away!"

Carlos walked toward her, and the chimeras pulled back like waves in his wake. Tentacles shot out from beneath Ophelia and headed straight for Carlos, slicing their skin and breaking their bones, piercing their side and burrowing into flesh. The impact caused the youth's thin body to stumble forward.

"Carlos…!"

Unable to watch any more, Oliver got to his feet, sword in hand, but Godfrey's tall frame blocked the way. He shook his head quietly at the confused boy.

"It's okay," Godfrey told him. "Let Carlos handle it."

His voice was full of faith and conviction. Oliver could say nothing to that, even as Carlos was still being attacked by the tentacles. They didn't even try to draw their athame and fight back. It was as if this was their duty.

"You're so hasty, Lia. Don't worry—I'll give you everything."

Carlos's tone was unfathomably kind. They pointed a finger at their throat, and suddenly, the tattoo around their neck unfurled like a ribbon and disappeared. Oliver's gut told him a seal had just been undone. He swallowed hard, and the singing grew louder.

See? There you are, silly. Crying all by your lonesome.

Too much crying and you'll drown in a sea of tears.

It was an oddly familiar lullaby, sung in simple Yelglish. With every verse Carlos sang, their surroundings wavered. Like gently untying a knot, this strange reality continued to unravel little by little.

But it's okay now. I'm here for you.

*   *   *

You're not alone anymore. I'll end your loneliness with magic.

"...This is..."

It wasn't a spell. This voice itself was filled with power; Oliver realized it had been enchanted somehow. But that alone didn't explain it fully. Carlos's voice was clearly working to nullify this world Ophelia had created. Their voice rang out clear and true, like a perfect counteragent to the Salvadori witchcraft.

"Wait..."

He felt a twinge of *divinity*. Suddenly, all the pieces of the puzzle fell into place.

Oliver recalled the party he and Pete had been invited to; Carlos had called it a gathering of *"students with sex-based magical traits."* Thus, it was only natural that their leader—Carlos—also possessed something that fit that description.

What if this singing voice was that something—this alto voice, frozen in time before puberty could take effect? Everyone could sing in this range as children, but most lost that pure, innocent quality once they matured. However, via certain methods, it was possible to maintain that range—and, with many hours of training, develop a magical element to it.

A castrato. Only by eliminating the masculine features while a child was young could this enchanted voice be produced. Its tone was sacred, innocent—the ideal counteragent to the various sorcery that utilized one's biological sex.

"Good day. Nice weather we're having."

Carlos recalled the day they first met her, in the garden of that dark, cold mansion.

"...Who are you?"

The moment they laid eyes on her, they felt as if they'd been stabbed in the heart.

This young girl was heavily pregnant—a child born into this world as a descendant of succubi, fated to perfect her family's witchcraft via her womb, unwillingly emitting this Perfume that drew men to ravage her—no wonder she felt unable to love or be loved in return.

"I could be a friend, if you like."

Carlos Whitrow had been dispatched to serve as Ophelia's safety valve. As a castrato, Carlos could keep her in check whenever her magic went berserk. And when she inevitably was consumed by the spell in pursuit of her magecraft, they would be able to kill her without fail. This was Carlos's duty as a mage, entrusted to them through their family's pact with the Salvadoris.

"Am I going to bear your child this time?"

That shocking question spoke volumes about the environment in which she'd been raised. To her, a male's sole purpose was to plant their seed within her womb. She could hardly consider any other possible interaction.

"Oh, no, honey. That's not possible for me."

"…? What the heck?"

So they explained it in no uncertain terms. Of course, she was confused at first. *That's fine*, Carlos thought. Little by little, they'd teach her that she wasn't some broodmare—that there were other ways of interacting with people. Because they would always be by her side.

Ah, but…

"But enough of that. So did you want someone to chat with or not, Princess Grumpy?"

If possible, they wanted to see her smile. They wanted this girl—designated as no more than a vessel for bringing life into this world—to obtain a happiness that made her glad to be born human. They couldn't help but hope it was possible.

In that moment, their personal hope formed, defying their family's orders. Carlos Whitrow's life—and fate—was now sealed.

*　　*　　*

"I'm sorry, Ophelia… I was by your side, yet I couldn't help you at all," said Godfrey, his voice echoing within the crumbling womb. His expression was filled with guilt and regret—but the next moment, he forced it into a smile. Not one of gloomy remorse but of sheer gratitude as he watched his friend's final moments.

"Good-bye, Carlos…my best friend."

Oliver could tell Godfrey was fighting hard to keep his voice from breaking. But it was no use. His throat quivered uncontrollably. Tears flowed from his eyes unabated.

Carlos knew better than anyone that Godfrey was not one to conceal his emotions. They flashed one last smile as bright as the sun.

"Yeah. Good-bye, Al."

After saying farewell to their dear friend, Carlos turned back to Ophelia and resumed their march. They'd resolved to be by her side to the end, and they proceeded without hesitation.

Open the door and come to me. I am your home.

Let's doze by the fireplace for a bit, until those puffy eyes subside.

Carlos's throat screamed in protest. Their ribs were cracked and broken, and white-hot pain spread from their lungs through their entire body. The more they sang, the more their body broke down from the inside. The seal on their voice had been broken, and they were singing at full power, transcending the limits of any normal vocalist. If they continued like this, their body would not survive the effort.

But they didn't care one bit. Their song, their flesh, their thoughts—everything they had existed for the sake of the girl shivering before them.

"Stay away… Stay awaaaayyy!" she screamed.

Her tentacles ripped through Carlos's flesh, broke their bones, and ravaged their thin body over and over. And yet—Carlos never stopped advancing. The tentacles weakened, as if uncertain about killing the person in their grasp. Was it because of the voice? Or was it because the voice belonged to Carlos Whitrow?

My heart shall envelop you, so cease your tears.

The final verse tied everything together. And the moment it passed Carlos's lips, their arms wrapped around Ophelia.

"...I'm sorry. I promised to make you smile, and I failed," they whispered in her ear. The tentacles around Carlos fell to the ground lifelessly; in their arms, they could feel her sobbing.

"...Are you...stupid? No one asked you to..."

Her voice shook as she berated her friend.

Carlos gently patted her on the head. "I love you, my Lia. I always have, and I always will. Forever and ever."

They revealed to her the feelings that had never wavered since the day the two of them met. Even now, in their final moments, Carlos remained steadfast. It was the greatest, most personal gift they could offer her.

"...I hate you..."

Ophelia refused to accept it happily. However, she didn't reject it, either. Like a rebellious child receiving a present from a parent, she reluctantly took it in her hands, eyed it suspiciously, then finally nestled it in her bosom.

"...Don't let me go," she begged, finally accepting Carlos's loving embrace.

The youth quietly nodded, gripping her as hard as they could—and began their sonorous hymn once again.

Undone by the voice, the closed-off world fell apart. The chimeras disintegrated into sand without a fight. It was a gentle death; the girl's long days of suffering, and the loneliness that had begun the moment she was born, were now over.

*   *   *

In a matter of seconds, Oliver and the others found themselves sitting in a daze back in the real world, in the middle of the swamp.

"Are you okay, Noll?!"

"Noll…!"

Out of the corner of his eye, he saw his cousins running over. Still, he remained silent.

"……"

He gazed, unfocused, at a pile of beautifully white sand on the ground. Mere moments ago, Ophelia and Carlos had stood there in an embrace. They'd lived in this world, formed a bond—and this was the final evidence of that bond.

Afterword

Hello, this is Bokuto Uno. Did you make it through to the end?

Such ends are not uncommon at Kimberly. You could even say this is a textbook example. And that is precisely why the events these six first-years witnessed could be in their not-so-distant futures, as well.

The things gained and lost on this latest adventure offer a glimpse of what will be gained and lost going forward. It depends on the individual to accept or reject this. Only one thing is certain: Not a soul can emerge unscathed so long as they continue on the path of the mage.

And thus, the curtain falls on our group's first year. After a short break, it will once again rise, and the second-year act will begin.

There will be new encounters and unforeseen threats, all of which our protagonists will navigate with their first-year experiences under their belts.

And amid these busy days—the time for *him* to don the mask and make his move will finally come to pass.

We are going deeper now... Take care not to be swallowed by the darkness.